/ **Serpent's
Tooth** /

A RINEHART SUSPENSE NOVEL

BOOKS BY SARA WOODS

Serpent's Tooth
They Love Not Poison
Though I Know She Lies
And Shame the Devil
Tarry and Be Hanged
An Improbable Fiction
Knives Have Edges

A RINEHART SUSPENSE NOVEL

Serpent's Tooth

SARA WOODS

HOLT, RINEHART AND WINSTON
New York   Chicago   San Francisco

Any work of fiction whose characters were of a uniform excellence would rightly be condemned—by that fact if by no other—as being incredibly dull. Therefore no excuse can be considered necessary for the villainy or folly of the people in this book. It seems extremely unlikely that any one of them should resemble a real person alive or dead. Any such resemblance is completely unintentional and without malice.

∧ Prologue

"I don't believe it," said Jenny Maitland, looking over her husband's shoulder. Antony looked up from the papers he was perusing and smiled when he saw the newspaper cutting that had caught her attention. She was staring down at it with a kind of horrified fascination.

BAKER'S DOZEN, said the headline baldly. There were some lines of print, and then the photograph: a thin little man and a stout, comfortable-looking woman with a baby in her arms, and ranged alongside them a long row of children, carefully graded as to height, from George (age seventeen) to Basil (age three). "Twelve of them," said Jenny in an awed voice.

"Not their own, though. Foster children," Antony pointed out.

"That only makes it more—more noble," said Jenny, and turned her eyes to the smaller picture, beside the first, of a slight, dark child with a wistful expression—*Stella (11) whose arrival in the Baker home has brought the number of their "family" to a baker's dozen. The Bakers are parishioners of St. Wilfred's Church, in Cargate, Arkenshaw . . . .* "It must be the brief Chris Conway sent you. What on earth is it about?"

"A nasty case, love. Murder."

"They don't look the sort of people—"

1

"Who does? All the same, you'll find both murderer and victim in that photograph." He picked up a pencil and circled the head and shoulders of the fifth figure from the left—a rather stocky youth, with hair that was probably fair, and a set, self-conscious expression. "That's my client."

Jenny leaned closer again. "But he's only a boy."

"Fifteen when that was taken, about two years ago. He killed his foster father, Alfred Baker, apparently in a fit of ungovernable rage," he added; and sounded pleased with the well-worn phrase.

"Is he mad?"

"That remains to be seen. On the face of it it's murder, no extenuating circumstances, but Chris seems to think . . . well, I don't know what he thinks, but I could tell he's worried."

"That poor woman. How will she manage?"

"She seems to be coping. Won't hear of splitting up the family, apparently. Well, she's fond of them, I suppose . . . if she can remember which of them is which," he added doubtfully.

"To the eye of love—" said Jenny, and turned away. "I think I wish you weren't going to Arkenshaw, Antony. Remember what happened last time."

"This is quite a straightforward case," Maitland told her. And for once in his life he was very nearly right.

2

∧ Thursday, 19th May

I

It was a fine evening, and it would be light for several hours yet; but in spite of this there was a feeling of time returned as he stepped from the train and felt the cold breath of wind from the moor sweeping through the gloomy cavern of the station. It was eighteen months since Antony Maitland had first set foot in Arkenshaw, and on that occasion, too, Chris Conway had been there to meet him; and there he was again, standing at the other side of the barrier and with the faintly worried air that had become so familiar since that first meeting. His expression cleared as he caught sight of Maitland, and a moment later, their greetings exchanged, they were walking towards the car.

Outside the station it was both lighter and warmer, though it would take more than a little sunshine, Maitland considered, to make the streets of Arkenshaw really gay. There were the tall, soot-encrusted buildings; the roadway inconveniently dissected by tramlines; the Imperial Restaurant, a forbidding-looking place; and the hideous Victorianism of the Midland Hotel. "I'm taking you straight to the prison," said Conway, halting in the midst of the home-going traffic while the car in front of him seemed to be nerving itself to take a right turn. "I thought you'd be sure to want to see our client straightaway."

"Yes, of course." He would have been much more interested in a drink at the moment, and the thought of the prison depressed him, but who was he to damp another man's enthusiasm? "How's Star?"

"She's grand." His tone was enthusiastic, but when Maitland turned his head to look at him he was still regarding the road ahead with frowning concentration. Conway had gray eyes and regular features and dark brown hair that might have been red when he was younger. A reliable chap. He said now, interrupting Maitland's meditations, "I'm glad you could come. This business of young Joe . . . it bothers me."

"I suppose you know the boy well."

"Well, yes, of course. He's been our office boy for more than a year. Nearer two years, really. I never thought . . . it seems entirely out of character."

"No signs of violence?"

"No. He's rather quiet, rather slow. They're an intensely respectable family, you know, and he's never shown any signs of breaking out of the mold."

"I see. Tell me about the Bakers. No children of their own?"

"Not one. But they've certainly compensated"—he grinned, and pulled up again, this time for a traffic light—"I suppose some people might say they've overcompensated for it."

"None of the children are adopted?"

"No. I don't expect they could have afforded to do it that way."

"You spoke of them as a family."

"That's how they're always regarded. For instance, four of the children have left school now and are working, but it never seems to have occurred to any of them to leave home."

"Do you know them?"

"I know Alfred by sight, of course. He was Foster's clerk . . . but you know that. And I know of the family, everyone in Arkenshaw does. The *Yorkshire Post* may not be interested, but the local paper is. And the Catholic press . . . those cuttings I sent you came from the *Universe*."

"How long has Joe been with them?"

"Since he was four years old."

"Is anything known of his real parents."

"The father died in a railway accident and the mother drank. I don't know if that's cause and effect or not. Anyway, the local council took Joe over, being in need of care and protection, or whatever the phrase is. The mother has died since then."

"Can we do anything with that?"

"I'm no psychologist," (an amateur one, like the rest of us) "but Joe seems completely—well, completely uninhibited when he talks about his own parents."

"Does he remember them?"

"He says he remembers his mother."

"With affection?"

"With complete indifference, I'd say."

"That brings us to the heart of the matter. Is there any doubt of his guilt?"

"None whatever."

"Was he seen committing the murder?"

"No, but one of the boys—Fred—was just outside the door. He heard it, if you see what I mean. But, really, that's immaterial; Joe's never tried to deny what happened."

"And as your brief says nothing of extenuating circumstances, I must suppose there are none."

"No."

"Then what—?"

"Because there's no reason . . . no apparent reason . . . why he should have killed him."

"I see. Is the boy mad?"

"As sane as I am. I've had him examined, of course; the psychiatrist talked about schizophrenia, but I wouldn't mind betting this is one case where the jury won't agree with him."

"The traumatic effect of early separation from his mother." *& FATHER*

"Dr. Naylor says No."

"There must be a reason for what he did, even if it isn't obvious." He turned his head to look out the window as the car drew up, this time to watch some undignified scrambling on and off a tram. "Is this Cargate we're in?"

"Yes."

"I thought I recognized it."

"I was just going to point out to you . . . the turning on the right just ahead is Cartwright Avenue, where the Bakers live, and that's St. Wilfred's Church on the corner."

"Opposite the chapel. Convenient if you change your allegiance. I take it you've asked Joe why."

"I have. He's both polite and sullen, if you know what I mean. And he absolutely declines to say."

"We can't go into court with a 'not guilty' plea and nothing to justify it."

"That's just it. I won't let Joe plead 'guilty,' which is what he wanted to do. I thought perhaps you might find out . . . he might even talk to you; people sometimes will to a stranger."

"He might, I suppose. I can't see any reason at the moment why he should. And if he doesn't?"

"We shall be at the prison in five minutes," said Conway. "Let's wait and see."

Wentworth Gaol is not a beautiful building; it has about it nothing to elevate the mind. Antony muttered, "Abandon hope—" as they drove into the courtyard, but Conway had his attention fixed on the business of parking, and ignored the comment.

Long, gray corridors, echoing to their footsteps; the rattle of keys as doors were unlocked and secured again carefully; they reached at last the interview room, with Antony's spirits at their lowest ebb. Chris Conway seated himself immediately at the end of the table facing the door, but Maitland stood by the window, looking out between the bars at the row of shops at the other side of Cargate. A stationer's shop . . . an ironmonger's . . . a greengrocer's . . . *and to show thy pity upon all prisoners and captives* . . . He did not turn until the door had opened and closed again, and he heard Conway's chair scrape back as he came to his feet.

The photograph had been a good one, of this member of the Baker family at least. (Hard to think of the boy by his own name. What was it, anyway? Hartley?) A little taller, perhaps, a little thinner than he had been two years ago. He had mouse-colored hair and eyes that were a very light, cold blue, difficult to associate with any passion. He responded to Conway's introduction politely enough, though when he said, "It was good of you to come," it sounded as if he meant exactly the opposite. Maitland sat down by the table until the other two had settled themselves, but he was up and back to the window before many minutes had passed. He was a tall man, dark, with a thin, intelligent face and a casual air that could be deceiving. "I suppose you're tired of answering questions," he said now, sympathetically.

"Yes, I am." (Conway was quite right, there was a

sulky look about his mouth). "I don't see what good they'll do, anyway."

"Let's say I have a weakness for getting information at firsthand. Tell me about your family."

"They're all right."

"Mr. and Mrs. Baker . . . what did you call them?"

"Mum . . . and Dad."

"Do you remember your own parents?"

"I remember my mother. Not clearly."

"What do you remember about her?"

"Just that she was there."

"What she looked like?" Joe shook his head. "The sound of her voice? Her perfume?"

"I don't remember. From what I've been told I daresay it was whisky." He seemed completely indifferent as he said this, and Conway's quick glance at Maitland said "You see!" as clearly as if he had spoken.

"And you've been with the Bakers since you were four years old?"

"That's right."

"Do you remember what happened when you first went to live with them?"

"Nothing happened. George was a bit stuck up, but I was glad to have Winnie to play with."

"Did you enjoy your childhood?"

That gave him pause. "I suppose I did," he said at last, as though grudging the admission. And then, "I didn't care much for going to school."

Well, that was one remark volunteered, though not a very informative one. "Would you say your foster parents were kind to you?"

This seemed to be something else he had never considered. He answered as he had done before, "I suppose they were."

"You were always on good terms with them?"

"I never thought about it. They were there."

"You obeyed them?"

"Well, if I didn't, there was trouble." He paused, and thought about that for a moment. "Nothing out of the way."

"Nothing to make you feel resentful?"

"I don't think so. I don't remember."

"Would you say, then, that your feeling towards them was one of ordinary affection?"

"I was grateful to them, if that's what you mean."

"I used the word 'affection.' "

"If you like it better that way."

"What about your brothers and sisters? Would you say the same degree of affection—or lack of it—applied?"

"I should think so. I couldn't say about the kids."

"You said there'd be trouble. What sort of trouble?"

"Mum'd give you a clip over the ear, and be done with it. But Dad would lecture on and on . . . fit to sicken you."

"Did you resent that?"

"No." He seemed to be considering this answer, and perhaps he found it inadequate. "It's how people are, isn't it? Well . . . older people."

"Disapproving?"

"That's right."

"Tell me about your brothers and sisters, then." He was fumbling in his pocket as he spoke and presently produced a tattered envelope with a list of names scrawled on it.

George (Todd), 19
Winnie (Bell), 17
Joe (Hartley), 17
Fred (Greenhalgh), 16
Stella, 13
Dick, 12
Kathleen, 10

Patsy
Michael ⎱9
Moira, 7
Mary, 6
Basil, 5
Tommy, 3

"George is the eldest, isn't he?"

"He's a bit set up with himself these days, being in the bank and all."

"The Northumbrian and Wessex?"

"Yes. I don't think so much of that for a job, myself."

Maitland smiled at him. "You prefer the law?"

"Not really. The job was all right"—he glanced sideways at Chris Conway as he spoke, half in apology—"but the police, well, they're out to get you, aren't they?"

"Unjustly?"

Even that didn't shake him. "I didn't mean that."

"And your brother?"

"George puts on airs, but he'll get over it, I daresay."

"What about Winnie?"

"Oh, Win's a good sort."

Maitland seemed to be having some difficulty in deciphering his notes. "She's in the office at Comstock's Mill, isn't she?"

"Yes, but—"

"But what?"

"I'd say she works harder at home than she does at her job."

"Housework?"

"Cooking, cleaning, washing up."

"Don't you all help out?"

"Well, sometimes, when Dad gets after us. Mum says it's woman's work. Young Stella gives a hand, of course. And Kathleen and Patsy, but they're so young they're

10

more trouble that they're worth, Win says." He paused again, and his expression clouded. "I don't see what's the use of all this. I'm guilty, aren't I? I'm not trying to deny it."

Chris Conway came out of his silence. "Mr. Maitland is here to help you, Joe."

"I don't see that anyone can. I don't see why they should want to." (He isn't sulky, thought Maitland, listening. He's out of his depth and very much afraid.)

"Just leave that to us, won't you?" Conway suggested.

"Well . . . all right. But—"

"How old is Win?" asked Maitland, forestalling another protest; though that was one of the few things he could read clearly from his list.

"Same as me. Seventeen. Exactly three months older, if you want to know."

"And after you comes . . . Fred, doesn't he?"

"Mr. Conway can tell you about him."

"Can he?"

"He's doing my job now, working for Mr. Bates. And I wonder how you can stick him, Mr. Conway. Him and his jokes."

"He certainly keeps us from feeling dull," said Chris carefully.

"He's a young pest. But that's really the lot, you know. The others are just kids."

"What about Stella?"

"She's only thirteen."

"The newest member of the family, isn't she?"

"Yes."

"How long—?"

"She came two years ago."

"I see. How do you all get along together? Do you fight among yourselves?"

"What do you think?"

"I think you probably do."

"Oh, well! George needs taking down a peg sometimes, I told you that. And as for Fred, he has to be kept in his place. And Win sometimes gets bossy, not that I blame her for that."

"When you started work, did you never think of leaving home?"

"No."

"Why not?"

"Oh, well . . . George had an idea about that, you know. I didn't want to start a fuss."

"George thought about leaving home at one time, but there was a fuss, and so he changed his mind."

"That's right. It wasn't like our own parents, was it? They didn't have to take us in."

"Well, now, you've been working for Mr. Bates, and Mr. Conway here, since you left school. What is your salary?"

"Eight pounds a week."

"Do you make a contribution at home?"

"I give—I gave Mum four quid every Friday."

"And you have to pay for your stamps and income tax, I suppose."

"Same as anyone else."

"Yes, of course. What are your recreations?"

"I like soccer, and I'm pretty good at swimming."

"Cricket?"

"Not now. I'm not all that good."

"Do you read much?"

"Quite a bit. Nothing serious. Adventure and such."

"What about your brothers? Do they share your tastes?"

"George is mad about cars. Of course, he can't afford one. Fred . . . well, Fred's good at all sports, to tell you the truth. Just seems to take to them naturally somehow."

"And the younger members of the family?"

"We all get caught for baby-sitting now and then. If there's nothing on the telly, I read to them; that's the easiest thing. Or we play cards if they don't feel like sitting quiet."

He was talking more easily now. Time to move in a little closer? "Was your foster father a violent man?"

"Not a bit of it."

"Did he drink?"

"Not to say drink. He liked a drop of whisky now and then."

"Tell me about the day he died."

"I don't want to talk about that."

"You regard yourself as an adult, don't you?"

"Yes, I do."

"Then you should be willing to abide by the consequences of your actions."

"Well, I am. I killed him, and I wish now I hadn't because it doesn't seem to have done any good. But I'm ready to—to pay for what I did."

"Before we come to the question of payment, there are things I want to know." Joe's mouth was set in a stubborn line. He didn't look at all amenable to any argument, however specious. "For instance, why did you kill him?"

"I had my reasons."

"Yes, I've no doubt of that. What were they?"

"I was angry, that's why."

"Do you normally feel murderous when you lose your temper?"

"I never felt that way before."

"Well . . . what reason had you?"

"That's nobody's business but my own."

"I am sorry to contradict you, Joe, but it is Mr. Conway's business, too . . . and mine."

"I don't want to sound ungrateful, but—"

"Let's not talk about gratitude," said Maitland quickly.

"Well, I'm sorry."

"But you won't tell me?"

"No."

"Tell me about that day, then. Tell me what happened."

"It was just a day like any other."

"A Sunday, wasn't it?"

"Yes." He hesitated a moment, and then shrugged as though it was too much bother to argue. "I went to early Mass with Mum and the kids. Win stayed behind to get the breakfast and went later with Dad. He was having a bit of a lie-in. So we all had breakfast together, and then we sat about and read the Sunday papers, only I happen to like the *People* better than the *Catholic Herald,* and Mum was trying to get me to change."

"Why did she do that?"

"Oh, well, she's always had an idea, you know, that I might go to the seminary."

"To study for the priesthood?"

"That's only what Mum thought. It wasn't my idea."

"No, I see. What happened after that?"

"I went out into the garden and bowled to Dick for a bit, and then we had dinner."

"The whole family together."

"Yes."

"Did anything happen? Was there any discussion . . . any dissension?"

"Not that I remember."

"And then?"

"I went for a walk."

"Alone?"

"No, Stella came with me. When we came back—"

"What time was that?"

"About half past four. I didn't really notice. And I went into the sitting room and Dad was alone there. And that was when . . . when—"

"When you killed him?"

"Yes."

"Just like that. No words between you?"

"We were talking . . . of course."

"Quarreling?"

"You could call it that."

"Was he angry with you?"

"We were both angry."

"Why?"

"I'm not going to tell you."

"What did you do then?"

"You know the answer to that."

"I know. I still want you to tell me."

"I picked up the poker and I hit him, and I suppose I hit him again."

"You don't remember?"

"Only . . . the first time." This time the pause was a long one. "And then Fred came in and took the poker away from me. and I saw what I had done."

III

They were at the prison for more than an hour, but Joe's story did not change. Only his speech became more ragged, as though he found the reiterated questions distressing; or perhaps he was having hard work keeping his temper. Neither Maitland nor Conway spoke until they were back in the car and Conway had turned into Cargate and was driving towards the town. Then Maitland said in an exasperated tone, "Look here, what *was* Baker like?"

Chris did not answer immediately, so that Maitland had time to think crossly that perhaps Joe's deliberate manner had been contagious. They had passed the second set of traffic lights before Conway said, "I only know of him, you see."

"Tell me that, then."

"Well, the newspaper took them up when they took in

the sixth child. It's a girl, I think, but I can't remember her name."

"Kathleen."

"Was it? The twins came next, Patsy and Michael, about a year later. After that there were fairly regular news stories, as the younger children came along, and last of all Stella, a couple of years ago. I've known Baker by sight ever since I was articled, of course—"

"I know he was a solicitor's clerk . . . I can't remember the chap's name."

"Herbert Foster. Baker seemed rather a colorless little man, perhaps he was different off duty. We didn't really have many dealings; Foster's clients are an exclusive bunch."

"I thought Jones and Ashby—"

"They have the businessmen. Foster has the county."

"I see. How did you come to employ Joe?"

"It was Mr. Bates's idea to take one of the boys, and give him his articles later if he showed any inclination. I'm not sure, but I think Father O'Brien suggested it to him. As it turned out several people had the same idea . . . that offers of employment might be welcome, I mean. George preferred the bank, so Joe came to us a few months later, when he left school."

"You'd agree with Joe about that, then . . . that Baker wasn't a violent man?"

"He certainly didn't give one that impression," said Conwas cautiously.

"I was thinking that perhaps Joe might have had some idea of protecting his mother . . . his foster mother, I should say. That's a story that always goes down well."

"Without Joe's cooperation . . . anyway, that isn't what Mrs. Baker says."

"What does she say?"

"She was upstairs and didn't know what had happened

16

until Win went up to tell her. As for the rest, there'd been no signs of ill-feeling between Joe and her husband, and she had no idea what could have set him off."

"Not very helpful."

"I'm afraid not." He hesitated. "What did you think of Joe?"

"He seemed to me both tolerant and good-natured. Not at all the sort of boy to run amok."

"That's a very fair estimate. I'd have said the same thing, up to now."

"That doesn't help, either," said Maitland gloomily. "Do you suppose there might have been some resentment? If he wanted to leave home, and didn't feel able to . . . he was giving them a fair proportion of his salary, too."

"I daresay they needed it. In any case, that's hardly an explanation, let alone an excuse."

"Oh . . . well."

"He seemed to be managing all right, anyway. He had ten pounds saved in the Post Office."

"Wealth beyond the dreams of avarice. As to why he did it, are we likely to get any enlightenment from the witnesses?"

"I shouldn't think so."

"Fred, I suppose, will be called by the prosecution."

"That's right. And Mrs. Baker. And Win."

"Who have we got?"

"Character witnesses . . . if we use them."

"Shouldn't we?"

"Not if we use Dr. Naylor's evidence. They'd cancel each other out."

"Yes, I see. Who's appearing for the prosecution?"

"Anderson."

"Oh, dear!"

Conway shot a glance at his companion. "Is he good?"

"His only fault is a tendency to repeat the same joke

over and over again. And that's not so bad in court . . . I mean, he makes his points with a sledgehammer. He may bore the jury, but he doesn't run any risk of their not understanding what he's at."

"And as we haven't got a defense—" It was Conway's turn to sound dismal.

"Come now, we haven't started yet," Maitland told him, cheering up as his companion became depressed. "Who's my junior?"

"I got Bushey again. I thought . . . you're used to each other."

"You mean, he's used to me."

"Well . . . if you like."

"That only leaves the judge then. Who have we drawn?"

"Gilmour," said Chris. He seemed about to add something, and then decided against it.

"That," said Maitland, "as you so carefully refrained from pointing out, is just about the limit."

"It's no use trying to put anything over on the court, with him up there asking questions," said Conway, rubbing it in.

"No. I say, where are we going," he added, as the car turned right into a street of modern houses. "This isn't the way to the hotel."

"Grandma's expecting us for supper."

"That's good. How is she?"

"Her hands are bad, but she manages fairly well. Star's gone round to help her."

"Has she forgiven you yet for being born under the wrong sign of the zodiac?"

Chris smiled. "I suppose you could say she's resigned."

"And Sergeant Duckett—"

"Didn't I tell you? He's an inspector now."

"I'm glad to hear it."

"He doesn't change much," said Chris. "And I'm in his

18

good books as long as Star is happy." He slowed, and signaled a right turn, and took it cautiously into a narrow lane with a high wall on one side and open ground on the other.

"I remember," said Maitland. "Waterworks on our right, and Old Peel Farm on our left. It still looks pretty lonely."

"They're starting to build at the other end of the lane," Conway told him, parking the car on the grass verge close beside the wall and waiting for Maitland to get out so that he could follow him. "It's a nice evening, isn't it?" he added, as they crossed the road, and looked surprised when Antony said,

"Chilly," and turned up the collar of his raincoat. They were on higher ground here than in the center of the town, and the wind from the moor was cold.

When he came to think of it, the kitchen at Old Peel Farm *was* Arkenshaw, as if the whole essence of the town was concentrated between its four walls. He knew the drill now, you didn't linger in the hall, "wasting the electric," but found a peg for your coat as quickly as possible and went through a door on the right into the warmth of the kitchen.

Star had let them in. Star Conway, who had been Star Duckett the first time he was in Arkenshaw and very uncertain in her mind as to what she was going to do with her future. He thought now that he had never seen a bigger change in anybody in his life. She wasn't very tall, and her dark hair was curly and not particularly tidy; what she had lost was her former gravity, and she had instead a sort of sparkling happiness that made Antony think even better of Chris Conway than he had done before.

The kitchen hadn't changed, though: the old-fashioned range was still as gleamingly black, the steelwork as burnished, the fire as bright, the furniture as uncompromisingly Victorian. Only the dragon vase had red tulips instead of chrysanthemums. Old Mrs. Duckett was just the same too, enthroned in her high-backed chair to the left of the hearth. She glared at the three of them as they trooped in and singled Maitland out for a greeting. "So you've come," she said, rather as though her worst forebodings had been fulfilled by the mere sight of him. "Haven't hurried yourself, have you? And Star with supper all ready and waiting."

"Now you know, Grandma," said Star firmly, "I told you they had to go to the prison first."

"Well, don't dillydally now they're here," the old lady retorted. "You'd best call your dad right away."

She was rather stout and stiffly erect as she sat there, her creamy-white hair drawn back into a bun, her cheeks softly pink, her eyes intensely blue. She put out a hand to take Antony's as he crossed the room to her side, and pressed it even while her voice scolded on. "Not a bit more flesh than you had the last time you were here," she said in a grumbling tone. Her eyes on his face were shrewd and a little anxious. From the stiff way he held himself she saw that he was tired, and probably his shoulder was painful, but she had learned better than to mention that. "I suppose it's living in London that does it," she said. "Godless place. And now you've let that Chris drag you here on a wild-goose chase. You ought to have more sense."

He knew her too well to be startled over what might have suggested an indiscretion on Conway's part. "I suppose the stars told you that," he said, and smiled at her, only to be told roundly that it was no laughing matter.

"*Do not embark on any enterprise involving a Piscean,*" said Grandma Duckett awfully, and transferred her glare to Chris Conway, who grinned at her weakly and shuffled his feet. "I remember quite well that you're Cancer," she added to Maitland in an accusing tone.

As usual, he was surrendering himself to the sheer pleasure of her company, the interlude at the prison for the moment forgotten. "You never quite believed I was telling you the truth about that," he reminded her.

"Oh, I believed you. Stands to reason a man'd know t' date of his own birth."

"But not the precise second," he said, teasing her, and was saved from one of her sharper retorts by Inspector Duckett coming into the room.

Antony couldn't recall that he had ever seen him out of uniform before, except at Star's wedding, when he had looked excessively uncomfortable in what was obviously borrowed finery. Now, in tweeds, he seemed larger than ever; but he wasn't on the defensive as he had been when first they met, his eyes had a milder expression, and only his sandy-colored moustache bristled with an effect of fierceness.

"Glad to see you again, Mr. Maitland," he said. But Grandma didn't give Antony time for more than the most formal rejoinder before she was bustling them to the table.

Supper at Old Peel Farm was a substantial meal: an excellent mixed grill, followed by tea and parkin. Old Mrs. Duckett encouraged conversation; her son was talkative and affable. Maitland found that he had slipped, during his absence, into the status of an old family friend, which seemed a comfortable thing to be. Chris was rather silent; it was amusing to see that he hadn't yet got over his awe of the old lady, though he seemed on easy enough terms with the inspector. Star wasn't ever a talkative girl, but she sparkled quietly and was obviously enjoying herself.

It wasn't until the meal was ended and Star was stacking the plates and Chris had gone into the scullery to find a tray that a momentary silence fell, and Maitland had the opportunity to ask, "Do either of you know the Bakers?" because as long as he was here there wasn't any harm in finding out . . .

"They're Romans," said Grandma, as if that was enough for anybody to know.

"I just thought—" he spread his hands in a vague gesture, but it was more than enough for the old lady.

"I don't hold with scandal and backbiting, Mr. Maitland," she told him austerely.

"Who said anything about scandal?" His eyes moved to Fred Duckett's face, and then back to Grandma again. "I want to do what's best for the boy," he added. She gave him a stony look.

"We don't know but what the whole town knows," said the inspector gruffly. "Barring t' fact that Alfred Baker was a conscientious type. A sight too conscientious, if you ask me."

"Now, what do you mean by that?"

"Oh, well, he'd explain things," said Duckett, rather as if this was an old grievance. "Over and over, when you'd got him right t' first time."

"You've met him in the course of business, I expect."

"Aye. I've seen him in t' Slubbers' Arms, too. A very temperate man," said the Inspector, watching his mother for any signs of protest. "Make a pint last the whole evening, he would, but there, I don't suppose he had much cash to spare."

"Who did he drink with? Who did he meet in the pub?"

"A man called O'Donnell. Claud O'Donnell. He's an estate agent."

"Another Catholic?"

"Aye, I daresay."

"What about Mrs. Baker?"

"I don't see what she's got to do with you, Mr. Maitland," said Grandma belligerently.

"No." He was vague again. "I want to understand them," he said.

"She's in C.W.L.," she told him grudgingly. "I've no doubt they mean well. Charitable work, and such."

"Catholic Women's League," Fred Duckett explained. "She'd go to church socials, too, I wouldn't wonder. A regular pillar of St. Wilfred's, as they say," he went on, so that Maitland had a sudden vision of the woman whose picture he had seen, a stout and unlikely caryatid. "But that's about all I can tell you about her."

"Then we come to the children." He rather expected Grandma to exercise her power to veto at this point, but surprisingly she was silent. "George is the eldest, isn't he?"

"Aye . . . well. There's no real harm in George," said Inspector Duckett, rather as if he were refuting a statement to the contrary. "A bit of a dandy . . . I'd make him cut his hair if he was my son. And fond of the girls, but nothing out of the way. Of course there was the time when he drove doctor's car round the block," he added, warming to his theme, "which he didn't ought to have done, him having no license, let alone permission to take it. But there, Doctor Ryder isn't one to make a fuss."

"You didn't hear of it in your official capacity, I take it."

"No, there was no complaint made. Larking about, that's all."

"You can't say even that much of Winnie," said Star. She put the last of the cups onto the tray Chris was holding and gathered up the cloth by its corners. "She's domesticated," she added, and went to hold open the scullery door.

"No boyfriends?"

"No time." Star smiled at him and followed her husband out of the room.

"That's true enough," said Duckett, nodding. Grandma had folded her lips, and there was something ominous about her silence.

"Tell me about my client, then. He's the one I'm most interested in, of course."

"Chris gives him a good character," said Grandma, before Inspector Duckett could speak.

"So I understand."

"That's reet enough," said the inspector, nodding his head.

"No criminal record," asked Maitland, smiling.

"Nowt o' that."

"The younger boy. The one whose evidence is going to convict Joe."

"That's none of t' lad's doing," said Grandma sharply.

"I realize that. Is he as blameless a character as his brothers?"

"A young devil, Chris says. Well, there've been complaints . . . Mischief Night fun that was carried a bit too far, that sort of thing. But everyone has a soft spot for the Bakers; they wouldn't carry through with it, once they knew."

"Like George, though . . . no real harm in him."

"None in the world."

There didn't seem to be much more that could profitably be discussed. Grandma thawed again when she saw he had come to the end of his questions. Chris and Star must be doing the washing up. They returned at last and took Antony back to the hotel in time to put in a belated appearance in the bar mess. Later, when he telephoned Jenny, he told her at length about the visit. "Grandma's a holy terror," he said. "She doesn't change at all."

"Give her my love," said Jenny. And then, "This time she won't be able to help you." And Antony laughed, and agreed.

"Except insofar as her deflationary tactics are good for my soul."

He believed what he was saying, but he was reckoning without Grandma Duckett. And that, as he should have known, was a foolish thing to do.

⋏ Friday, 20th May

I

The Assize at Arkenshaw is of very ancient date, and the courtroom, though comparatively modern, is damp, and drafty, and inconveniently placed in a room in the Town Hall which, on less solemn occasions, is used for dancing. Outside, in deference to the judge's known views, the road was closed to traffic, and a number of temporary "One Way" signs had been erected; so that the court sat in an atmosphere of frustration and general ill will that might have daunted a more sensitive man. Mr. Justice Gilmour, being by nature both pessimistic and contrary, thrived on it, and had even been known to say, when dining in the bar mess, that Arkenshaw was one of his favorite cities.

This morning, however, his mood was undeniably grumpy. He didn't like murder cases, and while he had nothing against William Anderson, who was appearing for the prosecution, he would have been decidedly happier if Antony Maitland hadn't been briefed by the defense. Counsel for the Defense had a reputation for being unorthodox, and though he had behaved with strict propriety throughout the one case he had conducted before his lordship, there was never any knowing what he might be up to next. Besides, he had a humorous look, which Gilmour mistrusted, and his respectful air might—just possibly—have an undertone of satire. As for the prisoner, he had pleaded "not guilty," so presumably they were going to try for a verdict of diminished responsibility, on one count or another. The boy looked sullen; it was hard in the circumstances to eye him objectively, and difficult to see what it was about the case that had attracted his counsel sufficiently to bring him two hundred miles north, away from the Old Bailey and the law courts, where most of his practice lay.

William Anderson, on the other hand, rather welcomed the opportunity of crossing swords with Maitland; particularly, it must be admitted, when he himself seemed to be presenting a cast-iron case. He knew his opponent slightly, as an amusing companion; he knew him a good deal better by repute. It would certainly be a triumph to get a conviction for murder, and there was no doubt about it, either, the verdict would be justified. In recent days these young people . . . his thoughts blended in with the words of his opening speech.

"—these young people have claimed, and have been given, a good deal of license. You may be inclined, ladies and gentlemen of the jury, to feel that the youth of the accused entitles him to your pity, but look for a moment at the other side of the coin—"

Chris Conway was listening with mixed feelings. He had a good deal of faith in Maitland's ingenuity, but he couldn't for the life of him see where it was going to get them in this case. Anderson was a large man, and undeniably an impressive figure in wig and gown. The trouble was, his subject matter was impressive, too.

"—freely accepted into their home," he was saying, "and given all the benefits of loving family life. It is unfashionable today to talk of duty, of gratitude, but are we therefore dispensed from the practice of those virtues? I think you will agree with me—"

Maitland was sitting in a relaxed position, with his legs stretched out in front of him, but Chris knew better than to think he was asleep. He was listening to Anderson with somewhat rueful admiration . . . the chap held all the cards, certainly, but—worse than that—he was obviously sincere. And why not? There was the weekend coming up, and perhaps after a day in court Joe Hartley might change his mind and explain. Failing that, there didn't seem much they could do, except play Chris Conway's psychiatrist for all he was worth, and neither Counsel for the Prosecution nor the judge was likely to let them get away with that. He hadn't had a chance to weigh up the jury yet, but in spite of what Anderson said, they'd be more likely to damn the prisoner because of his youth than to pity him.

Beside his leader, John Bushey was listening to the opening speech with genuine detachment. Of course, you never could tell with Maitland, he might surprise them all before they were through. But it seemed fair to say this wasn't his sort of case, an open-and-shut affair, with little room for maneuver and no room for surprises. Bushey was a solidly built man and belied his name by being almost completely bald. He was some years older than Maitland and inclined to view the younger man's wilder flights of fancy with an indulgent eye, being not without humor himself, though he preferred to base his own conclusions on a firm basis of fact.

It seemed likely that Anderson was reaching the end of his remarks. Maitland evidently thought so; he sat up and opened his eyes and fell to studying the jury. Eight men and four women . . . was that a good thing or a bad? They had the usual self-conscious look ("stuffed" he had been known to call it in his less charitable moments), and they'd mean to be impartial, he knew that, but most likely each one of them had made up his mind already. And for all that he could offer them . . . but there'd be time enough to worry about that later. It was a puzzle, all the same. A sensible boy, a sane boy . . . he had a great regard for Chris Conway's opinion. There must be some reason for what Joe Hartley did, and Maitland felt he would like the opportunity to judge for himself whether it was bad or good. He began to make a sketch of the foreman of the jury, on the back of his brief.

He was so preoccupied that he didn't realize at first that Anderson had finished and that the first witness had been called. This was the architect who had drawn a plan of the ground floor of the Baker's house, 10 Cartwright Avenue, and who was willing to swear to its accuracy before it was taken into evidence. Maitland had seen the plan already and didn't find it particularly illuminating. He looked up with more interest when the second witness went into the box.

Detective-Inspector Thorpe was a tall man, very thin, with a face that looked as if it had been hewn carelessly out of a particularly unyielding block of wood. He gave his evidence with a cautious air (Antony felt it was likely he had appeared before Mr. Justice Gilmour before), and his voice was as expressionless as his face, so that it would have been hard to fault him on the score of impartiality. "In consequence of a telephone call received at the station at two minutes past five o'clock on the afternoon of Sunday, the twenty-fourth of April, I proceeded to Cartwright Avenue—"

"To number ten, the Bakers' house?"

"Yes, sir. I was accompanied by Detective-Sergeant Appleyard, and closely followed by Detective-Sergeant Gleason, who was off duty and had to be called from his home."

"What did you find there?" Anderson's tone was studiedly

casual. Most likely he didn't care for what Maitland had once heard a judge call "the atmosphere of the note-book."

"I found the deceased, in the room marked 'living room' on the plan. He was lying—"

"Was he already dead?"

"Oh, yes, sir, no doubt about that," said Thorpe, relaxing a little. "He was lying on his back in front of the fire, but I found upon enquiry that he had fallen all of a heap like, and an ill-advised endeavor had been made to straighten him out. He appeared to have multiple injuries to the head—"

"Mr. Anderson," said the judge.

"My lord?"

"Will you not be calling medical evidence?"

"Indeed we shall, my lord."

"Then perhaps—" he waved a hand in the direction of the witness and sank back into his coma again.

"As your lordship pleases." He turned back to the inspector again. "What was the appearance of the room?"

"There were no signs of a struggle. Everything appeared to be in order. But there were bloodstains on the mantel, and on the hearth, and on the chair which stood on the left of the fireplace."

"Were you able to form any opinion at that time as to the weapon which had been used?"

"There was a heavy brass poker lying in the hearth, with traces of blood and hair. This was taken for testing. I then questioned the witnesses—"

"Who were present?"

"Mrs. Agnes Baker, in a state of great distress. Miss Winifred Bell. Frederick Greenhalgh. And the accused, Joseph Hartley. In consequence of what I was told I cautioned the accused and took him to the station, and his solicitor was sent for. Hartley was told that he was under no compulsion to make a statement, and he replied, 'I shan't.' And that was all he said, then or later," reported Thorpe with a trace of indignation in his tone that made him at once more human.

"By 'later' you mean, after his arrest?"

"Yes, I do."

"What was his demeanor all this time?"

"When I first saw him he seemed to be in a daze. Afterwards . . . I'd say he was just sulky."

Bushey turned his head at that, but Maitland was listening quietly and made no sign. "What was the condition of the prisoner's clothing?" Anderson asked, seemingly unconscious of this byplay.

"It was heavily stained, mainly on the front of the jacket, but some stains on the trousers, too. I have here the report from the forensic laboratory at Wakefield."

"Will you read it to us, Inspector?"

The report wandered obscurely from serological tests to agglutinins and agglutinogens, with passing references to the work of Landsteiner and Dungern and Hirschfeld. Maitland let his attention wander (he'd done his homework on the report already) until he heard Anderson suggest, "In plain terms, Inspector—"

"In plain terms, sir, the blood on the accused's clothing and that of the deceased were both type B, which as you know is comparatively rare—"

"In European countries it occurs with a frequency of eight point six per cent," said Anderson, with an eye on the jury.

"—and the blood of the accused is of the more ordinary type O."

"Does the report also cover the condition of the poker?"

"It does. The blood was also type B, while the hairs were identified as being similar to those of the deceased."

"Little doubt, then, that this was the murder weapon."

"To my mind, no doubt at all."

"Thank you, Inspector. I have no further questions."

Anderson seated himself, and Maitland came leisurely to his feet. "How long would you say elapsed, Inspector, between the call to the police station and your arrival at the Bakers' house in Cartwright Avenue?"

"Ten minutes. Twelve minutes, perhaps."

"No time, in fact, for any of the people present to have recovered from the shock."

"I suppose not."

"Mrs. Baker, you said, was in a state of great distress."

"Yes."

"Hysterical, perhaps."

"Inclined to be hysterical."

"Who telephoned the police station?"

"I understood it had been Miss Bell."

"And was she in a state of great distress, too?"

"She had been crying, I think, but she answered my questions very clearly."

"And the younger boy, Frederick Greenhalgh?"

"He couldn't stop talking."

"What did he say?"

"That he had been in the hall and heard the sound of the blow—"

"In something nearer his own words, Inspector."

"He kept saying how awful it was. No, 'ghastly' . . . 'it was ghastly,' over and over again. And he said he rushed in and his brother—the prisoner—was standing quite still with the poker in his hand, and he went over and took it away from him, and then he saw what had happened."

"I see. They all showed signs of shock, in their different ways. And my client, you say, appeared to be dazed."

"That's how it seemed to me."

"Do you know how old he is, Inspector?"

"He's seventeen."

"Not very old. Do you think a boy who had just knowingly, coldbloodedly, killed his foster father could have been so calm?"

"I'm only telling you how it was."

"Ten minutes . . . barely ten minutes after he had struck the blows."

"I don't know."

"But if he had no recollection of what had happened, if he was bewildered by the accusations that were made—"

"My lord!" said Anderson, getting up in a hurry.

The judge opened his eyes. "Mr. Maitland," he said, "the witness has made no claim to an expert knowledge of psychiatry."

"No, my lord."

"Then perhaps you will agree that this line of questioning is of little value."

"As your lordship pleases," said counsel noncommittally. He looked at the inspector for a moment and seemed to make up his mind. "Thank you. That is all," he said.

Anderson did not trouble to rexamine.

After that there was Detective-Sergeant Appleyard, another big man, but this time hefty with it . . . an athlete, most likely, who was just beginning to put on weight. He confirmed what the inspector had said, and neither Anderson nor Maitland, when he cross-examined, took him into the realm of conjecture. The only new thing to emerge was the evidence concerning fingerprints: there had been a number on the poker, blurred and indistinct, with Joe Hartley's clearly superimposed over all. Fred had gripped the poker farther down, where there were no prints but his.

The medical evidence came next. Alfred Baker had been struck four times, any one of the blows would have been of sufficient force to kill him. Maitland made no attempt to quibble about that, but he listened more carefully to the psychiatrist who was the next witness. Dr. Everett stated uncompromisingly, first in technical and then in everyday terms, that he had examined the accused, Joseph Hartley, and found in him no signs of insanity. When Anderson had finished his questions Counsel for the Defense got to his feet again.

"You say you saw the prisoner three days after his arrest, Dr. Everett, when you found him sullen and uncommunicative."

"That is correct."

"What behavior would you have expected to observe in a boy who felt himself to be unfairly accused?"

"I should have expected excitement, a vehement denial."

"You will be the first to admit, Doctor, that patterns of behavior vary greatly from case to case."

"Oh, certainly. But here I felt the pattern was not normal."

"You told my learned friend that you found no abnormality about my client."

"That is so. I meant, not normal for an ordinary, innocent man."

"I see. Suppose, Doctor, you had seen Joseph Hartley three days earlier, within half an hour, say, of the murder itself. What would you have expected to find?"

"Some violent reaction—"

"We have it from the Inspector of Police who was present that he was calm, in a daze."

"I was about to say, if he had any feelings of guilt. In all his time with me, the prisoner showed no sign of any such emotion."

There were more questions about that, of course, but when Maitland sat down he did not feel particularly pleased with the answers he had elicited. He was glad that Mr. Justice Gilmour came to life at this point and adjourned the court until two o'clock.

II

They went back to the Midland Hotel for lunch. Bushey was no more optimistic than his leader about the way the jury had taken the psychiatrist's evidence. "Damn all expert witnesses, anyway," he said cheerfully, observing Maitland's dejected look.

"We've got one of our own," said Antony, declining to be cheered.

"All but ours, then. I thought at one point you'd caught Everett out, but he made a good recovery."

"I think, on the whole, I shouldn't have pressed him. Ah, well, it can't be helped now."

"Did you see the *Arkenshaw Telegraph* this morning?"

"Should I have done?"

"They rather featured your connection with the case. Front-page stuff," said Bushey, either blind to or ignoring the tightening of Maitland's lips. (He didn't care for publicity, and a good deal of it—not always favorable—had attended his affairs, one way and another.) "You're not getting any ideas into your head, are you?" Bushey went on. "That young Joe might be innocent, for instance."

"Nothing like that." Maitland did not seem to resent the question. "I only want to know why the hell he did it."

"So do I," said Chris, putting down the menu and looking round for the waiter. "But I've got a feeling that's something we never shall find out."

III

The morning lethargy had left the court when it reconvened after the luncheon recess. Maitland was aware of a sort of simmering exitement as soon as he went in and was not altogether untouched by the feeling himself. The official witnesses—*deo volente*—were finished with; they would be coming to grips with the human problem now.

Mrs. Agnes Baker was neatly, if unimaginatively, dressed in a tweed suit and a brown felt hat that depressed Antony's spirits again as soon as he caught sight of it. She looked stouter than she had done in the picture he had seen and ill at ease in the strange surroundings. She repeated the oath in a nervous voice, clutching the Douay Bible that had been provided as if it might try to escape her, but she seemed to find Anderson's preliminary questions reassuring, and by the time he was finished with them she was answering readily enough.

"Now, Mrs. Baker, I understand that you and the late Mr. Baker had thirteen foster children."

"That's right."

"Can you tell me how long ago it is since the first of them came to live with you?"

"Just on seventeen years."

"That was George Todd, was it not? How old was he at the time?"

"Just two."

"And what was your reason for giving him a home?"

"He needed someone, and we hadn't any of our own. We'd have adopted him, see, but we couldn't afford that."

"And from time to time since then there have been other children who 'needed someone,'" said Anderson sympathetically.

"Yes, there have."

"Have you found it easy, Mrs. Baker, having so large a family dependent on you?"

"There's times I get tired. But it's worth it."

"And one of these foster children is the defendant, Joseph Hartley?"

She heaved a sigh at that, and nodded her head, and only said Yes as an afterthought.

"When did he come to live with you?"

"In 1953. He was four years old."

"And he has been in your care ever since?"

"That's right. Of course, the last two years he's been working."

"But still living at home."

"He's only seventeen, you know."

The judge leaned forward. "Does that mean, 'yes,' Mr. Anderson?"

"I believe, my lord . . . was Joseph Hartley still living with you at the time of your husband's death, Mrs. Baker?"

"Certainly he was."

"Will you tell us something about his character?"

"I don't quite—"

"Did he fit in well with the other members of the family?"

"There were only George and Winnie when he came. He took a bit of settling down, you know. After that he was all right."

"And his character? His disposition?"

"He was always willful. But good with the little ones, I'll say that for him, when he got older."

"Did he give you, or your husband, any cause for complaint?"

"Nothing special. Nothing out of the way."

"He was on good terms with his foster father?"

"Quite good terms."

"Can you think of any action of your husband's that might have aroused in him some feeling of resentment?"

"Alfred was good to all the children. He was no different with Joe."

"There was, so far as you are aware, no cause of dissension between them."

"None at all." She sighed again and began to fumble in her pocket for a handkerchief.

Anderson paused. Now he's coming to it, thought Maitland, but his attention was concentrated now on the witness. Bunched gray curls under the brown hat; a round face, and a rather high complexion; eyes that, even in the indifferent light of the courtroom, were quite startlingly blue. A kind woman, a motherly woman, an inarticulate woman, whose world had come crashing about her ears less than a month ago. And now Anderson was going to take her back . . .

"I am sorry to distress you, Mrs. Baker, but I must ask you to cast your mind back to the twenty-fourth of April, the day your husband died. Will you describe to us the events of that day?"

"I suppose I must."

"I am sorry, madam—"

"No, of course, I understand." But she dabbed her eyes furtively before she went on. "I took the children to eight o'clock Mass, and Joe came too. After we'd had breakfast Win and her Dad went to the eleven. and Stella and I washed up and I got the dinner started. I don't remember what they all were doing, but Joe was sitting by the fire in the kitchen, and I had to speak to him because he was reading some trash or other, when he might have been reading a nice story, or the *Universe*, or perhaps the *Catholic Herald*. So after a bit he went out with Dick, and I heard them in the garden, playing at ball. I had to call them twice when dinner was ready."

"Mr. Baker was back by that time?"

"Oh, yes. The eleven's always out by five to twelve, and we don't have Sunday dinner until one o'clock."

"So you were all together. Do you remember anything of the conversation?"

She smiled at that, a rather watery smile Maitland

thought it. "With thirteen of them you don't have conversation."

"No, I see. But perhaps you can tell us whether Joe— whether Joseph Hartley and Mr. Baker seemed to be on easy terms."

"If they weren't, there was nothing to show."

"And then—?"

"Well, we always like to have some idea of where they're going. George was meeting a friend of his, and Joe said he was going to take the tram out to Lane's End and go for a walk on the moor, and Stella said, 'Can I come, too?' There was the washing up, of course, but Winnie said, quick like, 'Kathleen and I will do it,' so Stella went with Joe."

"And the others?"

"Alfred liked to have a sleep of a Sunday afternoon. He went into the sitting room and shut the door. The children . . . well, they'd be between the playroom and the garden. I went upstairs to have a lay-down." She said all this without any apparent emotion, but now her voice faltered. "That was the last time I saw Dad, you see."

"The last time you saw your husband?"

"Yes, well, I mean, when he was alive."

"Do you know what time the accused returned from his walk?"

"No. I didn't know anything until Winnie came up to me, and then . . . well, I wasn't noticing the time."

"After Miss Bell had spoken to you, you went downstairs?"

"Of course I did. She wouldn't let me go into the sitting room, but the door was a bit open, and I could see Joe just standing there, and after a bit Fred came out. And then the police came." She paused, and for a moment Maitland was convinced that she was not aware of the crowded courtroom or of his learned friend, Mr. Anderson, waiting courteously for what she had to say. "I was . . . upset, you know. Not noticing much that went on. But after a while they took Joe away."

Maitland, when his turn came, was very brief. If ever a witness needed handling with kid gloves, that witness was Mrs. Baker. He wasn't at all sure the jury wouldn't object to his asking her any questions at all, but he thought he ought to risk it. "You have told us that my client was on good terms with your late husband."

"Yes." She was wary again.

"Can you tell us a little more clearly what you meant by that statement?" He hoped his tone was reassuring, but it was hard to tell.

"They didn't have much to say to one another. Joe's fond of sports, things like that. Alfred was more intellectual."

"Yes, I see. There was no tension between them. Nothing to suggest—"

"I never would have believed it. Never." She was dabbing her eyes again. "It's the ingratitude that hurts me," said Mrs. Baker, sniffing. "After all that we've done for him, Dad and I."

If Maitland thought this was rather an odd way of putting things ("I don't so much mind him killing my husband—"), he made no sign. Years of practice in the courts had taught him, if nothing else, that what people say often bears very little relation to what they really mean. "Had you ever had occasion to be afraid of Joseph Hartley's temper?" he asked, with much the same solicitude in his tone as Anderson had used.

"He was never a bad-tempered boy."

"Never?"

"Never that I saw," said Mrs. Baker firmly. He thought he couldn't do better than that, and thanked her, and let her go.

IV

Winifred Bell wasn't a beauty. She had straight, almost black hair and a snub nose, but her complexion was lovely. "Wholesome" was the word that came into Maitland's mind, and that seemed unkind, but he couldn't think of a better one. She was neatly dressed in a navy blue suit that might have been part of a school uniform, and a black velour hat that undoubtedly had been. Her hands were clenched tightly in front of her as she answered Anderson's questions about her name, and age, and habitation; in fact, her whole body was tense, and it was only gradually that she relaxed under his careful handling.

"Now, Miss Bell, I must ask you about the day your foster father died. The whole family was assembled at lunchtime?"

"For Sunday dinner, yes."

"I am afraid, Mr. Anderson—" said Gilmour, rousing himself again.

"If you would speak up, Miss Bell, so that we can all hear you."

"I just said yes."

"Do you remember the occasion clearly?" The witness nodded and muttered an agreement that again was almost inaudible. "Can you tell us what you talked about?"

"Mum wanted to know what our plans were for the afternoon."

"Can you remember Mr. Baker's part in the conversation?"

"Not really. He wasn't one to say much."

"Was he a good-tempered man, would you say?"

"Oh, yes."

"And on that day was his mood as usual?"

"I think so."

"He didn't seem put out in any way?"

She frowned over the question, and then said, "No," but with some hesitation.

"You seem doubtful about that, Miss Bell."

"No, I'm not. Not really."

"You didn't feel he was displeased about anything? Displeased with the prisoner, perhaps."

"Well, he did ask Joe, sharplike—when he didn't answer Mum right away—what he was doing with himself that afternoon."

"Why was that, do you think?"

"My lord!" said Maitland.

"I do not think, Mr. Anderson," said Gilmour, promptly enough to discount any idea Counsel for the Defense might have had that he was half-asleep, "I do not think we can properly ask the witness for her opinion." But Winnie replied, as if neither of them had spoken,

"There was a boy he didn't like Joe going out with."

Anderson glanced apologetically at the judge and waited for a moment, as though in hopes of getting permission to follow this promising byway. Receiving no sign, he went on smoothly, "What reply did Joseph Hartley make?"

There was another delay while Winnie worked her way back to the original question. "He just said he was going for a walk." Her hands were twisting together again, but she was speaking more clearly now. "And Dad said, 'Who with?' and Joe grinned at him and said, 'Stella, if she'll come with me,' and Dad didn't ask him any more then."

"He seemed satisfied with the reply?"

"Yes, I think so."

"And did the accused seem to resent the question in any way?"

"Not really," said Winnie, before Maitland could open his mouth to protest; which made him glad he hadn't done so. Anderson seemed to be half-inclined to press for a more

41

satisfactory answer, but after a pause he settled for a change of course.

"What did you do after dinner?"

"There was the washing up, and then I was reading."

"In the playroom?"

"I stayed in the kitchen, by the fire. It was quiet in there."

"Did you see the accused return from his walk?"

"Yes, they came in the back way. Their shoes were muddy, you see."

"Did you at that time observe any signs of anger?"

"No. I was reading."

"What happened after that?"

"Joe went out."

"Out of the house again?"

"No. I meant out of the kitchen. Stella stayed for a little while, warming her hands, and then she went away, too."

"And then?"

"I stayed where I was, reading." Her voice had dropped to a whisper again, but Anderson said, "Please speak up, Miss Bell," before the judge could interfere. "I stayed where I was, reading," she repeated, and stood quietly for a moment, staring down at her hands as though fascinated by the way they were writhing together. "And then I heard a dreadful sound."

"What kind of a sound?"

"A sort of a thumping. At least, it didn't seem dreadful then," she went on very quickly, "but afterwards . . . when I knew . . . I can't get it out of my head."

"What did you do then?"

"I wondered about it, so I went out into the hall, and Freddie was just coming out of the playroom. He pulled the door to behind him and went across to the sitting-room door."

"Was that closed, or open?"

"Closed. He didn't knock or anything. He just went in. And I heard him say something, only I couldn't tell what it was, and after a minute or so he came back to the door."

"Yes, Miss Bell."

"With—with the poker in his hand. And he said, 'Will you telephone for the doctor, Win? I think Dad's dead.' And it didn't sound like a joke, but I thought it must be, so I went to the door and looked in."

"I know this is difficult for you," Anderson told her, "but I must ask you what you saw."

"I saw Dad, and when I did I knew Freddie was right. He was lying all of a heap, and I didn't think that was very nice, so I tried to straighten him out a bit and Freddie came to help me. But then Joe said—"

"What was Joseph Hartley doing all this time?"

"He was just standing there, not three feet from where Dad was lying, with his hands hanging down by his sides. It was as if he wasn't there at all. And then he said, 'You oughtn't to touch anything, you know,' and I went away to phone the doctor. And the door of the playroom was still shut, so I went upstairs to tell Mum."

"Thank you, Miss Bell. That is all I wished to ask you."

She had already turned to go when Maitland's voice stopped her. "I'm sorry, Miss Bell. I won't keep you long." Poor child, he thought, as she turned to face him, she's had just about all she can take. Carefully, then . . .

"You told my friend"—he indicated Anderson with a gesture—"that you did the washing up and then spent the afternoon reading. What happened to the rest of the family?"

"Mum was lying down, and Dad was in the sitting room. George had gone out, and Joe and Stella, of course. The rest of them were between the playroom and the garden. Freddie was baby-sitting that afternoon."

"I see. Now there is something about which I should like you to go into a little more detail. When Mr. Baker asked my client about his plans for the afternoon, you say that Joseph did not seem to resent the question in any way."

"We were all used to it."

"Used to being asked where you were going and what you were going to do?"

"That's right."

"Please tell me exactly what happened."

She stood a moment, frowning at him. "Joe said he was going for a walk and would take Stella with him if she'd like to go. He always had a soft spot for Stella. Mum said, 'What about the washing up?' and I said Kathleen would help me."

"You wanted Stella to go with Joe."

"I thought it would set Dad's mind at rest. You see—"

Anderson came to his feet with a pained expression. The judge shook his head and said, "Mr. Maitland—" (It sounded more like a groan than anything else.) Maitland said, "As your lordship pleases," and held up a hand and smiled at the witness as her voice trailed into silence. "So you and Kathleen did the washing up."

"Dick helped, too. You see, Joe had made a deal with him"—for the first time she looked directly at the prisoner; then her eyes came back to counsel's face again—"he'd made it a condition, sort of, that if he bowled to Dick in the morning, Dick would help with the washing up."

"That was thoughtful of Joe, wasn't it?"

And suddenly her smile was warm and friendly, and she said, "Oh, *yes!*" with all the emphasis he could have wished. And then the memories came crowding back to her and she said, "Joe's like that . . . kind," in a shamefaced way, and stumbled as she left the witness-box a moment later.

V

Frederick Greenhalgh looked unnaturally solemn as he took the oath. He was a round-faced boy, not very tall for his sixteen years, with curly dark hair and an air of guile-lessness that was probably misleading. Unlike his foster sister, he spoke out clearly enough, but he seemed uneasy in his role as the prosecution's principal witness.

Anderson went through the preliminaries with the speed of long habit. The boy was vague about what had happened at the dinner table. There'd been some talk about plans, but he hadn't joined in; his afternoon was already fixed, keeping an eye on the kids. As far as he knew Joe had gone straight out when the meal was over. Maitland began to draw a small, incongruously cherubic devil on the pad in front of him.

"Please tell us what happened later in the afternoon of the same day, April twenty-fourth."

"Well, I was in the playroom all the time until twenty to five. I know the time because I was wondering how long to teatime. I mean, enough's enough, and I was getting pretty tired of the kids by then. There's a cloak-room down the hall, and that's where I was going when I heard the—the noises from the sitting room."

"Can you describe to us what you heard?"

"First there was a sort of strangled cry. I wouldn't have known it was Dad's voice if it hadn't been for what came after. And then there was a series of thuds. I don't know why, but straightaway it worried me."

"What did you do?"

"I went to see what was up."

"We should like to know in detail—"

"I was half-way down the hall, so I went across to the sitting room door, and opened it, and went in."

"And then?"

"It was ghastly. There was Joe standing on the right of the hearth with the poker in his hand and—and blood on it. And Dad—"

"I am sorry to have to press you for these details."

"He was lying on the rug, and his head was all bloody. When I got nearer I could see—"

"What could you see?"

"The damage the blows had done. It was ghastly. I couldn't believe he could be still alive. I'm sure he wasn't."

"Was the room disordered in any way?"

"No, not at all. There was just a newspaper, on the floor by Dad's chair."

"Was any window open?"

"No, they were all closed."

"So what did you do?"

"I took the poker from Joe. It seemed to be the best thing. It was bloody, too, and when I looked at it closely there were hairs on it."

"Did you notice anything about your—about the prisoner's condition?"

"He was . . . all spattered with blood, down the front of his jacket."

"Did you say anything to him?"

"I don't think so. I don't really know."

"What did you do?"

"I went back to the door and told Win, and she looked in . . . well, I told her not to. And then she went away to telephone. I wanted to be sick, as a matter of fact, but I thought someone ought to stay there. I didn't know what to do, really."

"You seem to have behaved with great presence of mind," said Anderson graciously. "What did the prisoner do while all this was going on?"

"He just stood there. And afterwards—after Win had

gone—he flopped down into the chair behind him. It looked as if he couldn't stand up any longer."

"Did he say anything?"

"Only that we shouldn't move things round."

"And did you?"

"No, of course not. Only to shift Dad a little. Win seemed . . . Win was upset."

There were repetitions, of course. It was all the same, Maitland reflected, shading in the imp's horns: a good story told in the bar mess, a good piece of evidence produced in court, and in either case *ad nauseam*. It seemed an age before Anderson sat down again, and Maitland was free to make what he could of the witness . . . which wouldn't, he expected, be very much.

"You say you left the playroom to visit the cloakroom. Did you close the door behind you?"

"Yes."

"Are you sure of that?"

"Yes, I am. If Dad was napping, he wouldn't want to hear the kids carrying on."

"I see. And you were already in the hall when you heard the first sounds from the sitting room."

"I don't think I could have heard anything, with both doors shut. But I remember quite clearly . . . I was halfway down the hall towards the cloakroom when I heard Dad cry out."

"I agree with you that it was probably Mr. Baker, but you told my friend that you couldn't recognize the voice."

"Well, I couldn't. But I'm sure—"

"Yes, thank you. Where were you when Miss Bell came out of the kitchen?"

"Just outside the sitting-room door."

"Miss Bell is under the impression that you had only just left the playroom."

"She's wrong, then." He paused, and then added earnestly, "I've thought about this, you know. I'm quite sure I'm right about where I was."

"Thank you," said Maitland again. A nicely brought up youngster, doing his best with a difficult assignment. It seemed a shame to plague him with questions. "So you opened the door and went in."

"Yes, I did."

"Were you surprised at what you saw?"

"I was flabbergasted," said Fred emphatically, after a moment's search to find the best word to express his emotions.

"Flabbergasted?" said Gilmour, a little peevishly. It had been a long afternoon.

"Surprised, my lord. Extremely surprised." When the judge did not seem to have anything more to say, Maitland turned to the witness again. "Were you surprised because Mr. Baker had been hurt, or because Joe was holding the poker?"

"Well, both, of course."

"Did my client resist when you took the poker from him?"

"No, not at all. He was just standing there," said Fred, as if in some way this constituted a grievance, "and he didn't actually hand it to me, but he didn't try to hold onto it at all."

"What did you do with the poker?"

"I laid it down in the hearth when I went to help Win."

"Would you agree with the police inspector that Joe seemed dazed?"

"I thought he seemed as if he was sleepwalking." He thought about that for a moment and then added, "Except that he was standing still."

"He spoke to you once, you said."

"Yes, but that didn't make any difference. He still sounded as if he wasn't all there."

"Thank you very much," said Maitland, suddenly cordial. "I have no more questions."

Anderson reexamined briefly, but the judge was restless by then and adjourned the court as soon as counsel sat down.

VI

Half an hour later, in Bushey's chambers, the defense team were met in conclave. Chris Conway was tense and unhappy; Bushey was getting his pipe going and seemed immersed in the task; Maitland stood by the window and looked out at the gray, but sunlit street and a fading advertisement for Typhoo Tips painted on the opposite wall and thought that the moors beyond the town would be a better place on a day like this than a room that smelled of stale smoke already, and was going to smell even worse when Bushey had completed his incendiary task.

"Well, we didn't get much joy out of that," said Chris disconsolately.

Antony did not move from the window. "Did you expect to?"

"Not really. No, of course I didn't."

"Hope springs eternal—" said Bushey, between puffs. He looked from one of his companions to the other and seemed to find something amusing in the situation. "We've the weekend before us," he added encouragingly.

Conway didn't seem to find the thought comforting. He looked at Maitland's back and said hesitantly, "I suppose it was stupid to think—" and then broke off, as if he had forgotten where the sentence was supposed to lead. Maitland made no direct reply, but after a moment he turned his head and asked,

"Why should Stella and Joe being together set Dad's mind at rest?"

"I can't imagine," said Chris shortly.

"Winnie said it would, if you remember."

"Yes, of course I remember. I can't see that it has anything to do with the case."

"How do you know that?" He turned to face the room as he spoke, but stayed where he was, leaning back against the paneling.

"Well, I don't, I suppose."

Bushey blew out a cloud of smoke. "It sounds to me as if Master Joe had been getting into bad company," he said.

"That's what I thought."

"It's all very well, but it doesn't help," Chris pointed out.

"All the same, I should like to know."

"If you're right, it's not likely to help the defense."

"I think we must know all we can about Joe Hartley before we go into court on Monday."

"Close as a clam, isn't he?" said Bushey. "Perhaps he'll open up when Anderson gets after him."

Chris started to say, "That's what I'm afraid of," but Maitland interrupted, saying quickly,

"We shan't be calling him."

There was a moment of almost complete silence. Bushey puffed at his pipe; his eyes were on Maitland now, they were bright with interest.

"But we've got to," said Chris, in despair.

"Under what compulsion?"

"Well . . . I mean . . . what will people think if we don't?"

"I'm more concerned with what they will think if we do. They'll certainly think he's sane," Maitland went on, "so what would be the use of our trying to persuade them that he was mentally unbalanced for about thirty seconds on the afternoon of April twenty-fourth?"

50

"I don't agree," said Conway. But he spoke without any real conviction.

"I daresay you don't, but you'll let me have my way . . . won't you?"

"I suppose it's no use arguing."

"Not a bit."

"What do you think?" Conway appealed to Bushey, who took his pipe out of his mouth long enough to say,

"Settle it between you."

"We might as well throw in our hand right away," said Chris hopelessly.

"Not just yet. I want to know more about Alfred Baker."

"I don't see how that will help."

"No, but I'm beginning to dislike him; he seems to have been such a ruddy paragon."

"I told you—"

"Yes, I know. I want to talk to his employer, and some of his friends, and the parish priest you mentioned. And then I want to talk to George, and Dick, and Stella. And *then* I want to talk to Joe again."

"Is that all?" said Chris, somewhere between bewilderment and exasperation.

"All I can think of for the moment. One thing may lead to another, of course."

"Do you really think so?"

"Can you manage? Am I asking too much of you?" asked Maitland, suddenly formal. He had a private theory that Chris Conway knew everything, at least where Arkenshaw was concerned, but it occurred to him for the first time that perhaps his demands might be regarded as a trifle exacting. Chris raised his hands in a gesture obviously designed to express both dismay and resignation.

"I can manage, all right. Let's hope it will do some good. May I use your telephone, Bushey? I'll call Herbert Foster now."

Herbert Foster lived in a rambling old house on Temple Street. He was a big man, with a head that looked too small for his body. He received Maitland and Conway in his study after dinner, a pleasant room with old, well-polished furniture and deep leather chairs. There was a spread of papers on the desk, as though he had been busy until the visitors were shown in, and Chris was inclined to be apologetic.

"I don't think we need to keep you very long," he said but carefully refrained from looking at his companion for confirmation of this statement.

"No hurry. No hurry at all," said Foster, waving them towards two of the more luxurious-looking chairs. But his eyes lingered on the desk for a moment before he followed them over to the hearth; the day's sunshine notwithstanding, the evening was chilly. "Have you had any dealings with the Imperial Insurance Company, Chris?"

"No," said Conway, his tone mildly enquiring.

"I'm finding them difficult. Very difficult. One of my clients—" He broke off, shaking his head. "The truth is, I miss Alfred a great deal. He used to deal with all these insurance claims for me."

"Yes, I'm sure you must miss him." Chris sounded awkward. He was wondering bitterly how much longer Maitland would choose to efface himself. "It was about Mr. Baker that we wanted to talk to you."

"Of course." He sat down and stared into the fire. "I've heard of you, Mr. Maitland," he said, still not looking at either of his visitors, so that he did not see Antony's quick frown. "It's right that Joe should have the best representation, of course, but do you really think you can help him?"

"That is something I'm trying to find out."

"I didn't know the boy well, you realize that." He paused

and added almost fretfully, "I can't think what possessed him to do such a thing."

"I can't, either. That's why I've come to you. I want to know all you can tell me about Alfred Baker."

"About *Alfred*," said Foster, as though the idea was new to him. "I can't tell you anything that will help you, I'm afraid."

"How long had he worked for you?"

"Thirty-two years. He started as office boy, when my father was still alive."

"How old was he when he died?"

"Forty-nine . . . no, fifty. He had a birthday the month before."

"I don't need to ask you whether you found him a satisfactory employee."

"Most certainly I did." He hesitated, as though wondering how much it would be proper for him to say. "In case you're in any doubt, I should add that he was a good man, Mr. Maitland."

"So I am told." His tone was flat, with no hint either of agreement or of scepticism. "Perhaps you could tell me in a little more detail—"

"He was, I think I should say, deeply religious. I found him loyal and conscientious, and if you know about his family, I needn't add that he was kindhearted and generous, as well."

"No, you don't need to add that." The idea seemed to depress him, but after a moment's reflection he smiled. "In addition to all that, I suppose he and Mrs. Baker would have qualified for the Dunmow flitch."

"I don't suppose it would ever have occurred to them to apply for it," said Foster seriously.

"No, but . . . never mind that. What were his relations with the rest of the family?"

"I think he worried about George sometimes . . . that's

the eldest boy, you know. Not that I imagine there was any harm—"

"What did George do?"

"From what I gather, he's fond of the girls. No harm in that, at his age. And a bit too conscious of his personal appearance . . . that sort of thing. And Alfred did say to me once that he wondered if it had been a mistake to take in a child of Stella's age . . . she was eleven when her parents died, you know."

"What was the trouble?"

"She was rather nervous, didn't seem to settle down as he had hoped she would."

"If those were Baker's worst worries—"

"I never heard him say a word about Joe."

"Do you mean that literally, or just that he didn't complain of him?"

"Oh, he spoke of him now and then. For instance, he consulted me when the question of a job came up. But nothing that could explain what happened. I should have said—wouldn't you, Chris?—that Joe was a very steady young fellow."

"Then why do you think—?"

"It's quite inexplicable to me."

"If he's sane, there must be some reason."

"You're implying that he's out of his mind."

Maitland smiled again, without much amusement. "If I thought I could get a jury to believe that, I shouldn't be worrying you now. What did you pay Baker, Mr. Foster? If you don't mind my asking."

"Twenty-four pounds a week."

"Gross?"

"No, I'm sorry. I mean that his take-home pay was about that."

"Do you know anything about his expenses?"

"Food and clothing would be the main ones, I think.

Mrs. Baker tells me he gave her twenty pounds each week. The house is owned by a man called O'Donnell—Claud O'Donnell—and in the circumstances I very much doubt if he charges them an economic rent."

"You mean, because of the size of the family?"

"That's what I had in mind."

"It makes me wonder how Mrs. Baker is managing now." Maitland made the remark diffidently and was surprised when Herbert Foster replied, this time without any hesitation,

"I'm allowing her the same amount. As a temporary measure, of course. Meanwhile, I've put in an application to the National Assistance Board on her behalf. I don't anticipate any real trouble there."

"That's good. So Alfred kept about four pounds for his personal expenses. Would he have to pay the rent out of that?"

"No, Mrs. Baker managed everything, she tells me. That's the normal thing in this part of the country, Mr. Maitland."

"I see."

"In any case, he can only have spent a fraction of it. He had over three thousand pounds in one of the Trustee Savings Banks."

"Did he though?"

"Yes. I admit I was surprised when I heard of it."

"Perhaps they banked part of the children's allowances."

"No, Mrs. Baker told me quite distinctly . . . she could hardly have managed without them, could she now?"

"I suppose not. We must add abstemiousness to Baker's other virtues, it seems."

"I think you could certainly do that." He glanced at Chris as he spoke, a doubtful look. Perhaps he was wondering whether Conway was responsible for the long list of questions.

"How much do the children's allowances amount to?"

"I really don't—"

"Thirty pounds. nine shillings, and sixpence a week," Chris put in.

"Exactly?" Maitland turned his head to smile at him. Conway nodded.

"They don't get anything for George, or Winnie, or Joe since he passed his seventeenth birthday. The other amounts are graded, and Mrs. Baker would have to buy clothes and provide pocket money out of the total, as well as food."

"Yes, I see." He looked back at Herbert Foster again. "That leaves us with his hobbies."

"I believe he was a keen chess player."

"Do you know anything about his friends?"

"Not really. A man called Rawdon seemed to be looking after things for Mrs. Baker . . . the funeral, and so on."

"That's all then." He came to his feet as he spoke. "Unless you can think of anything—anything at all—that might have given Joe Hartley a motive for what he did."

"If I could have thought of anything like that, I'd have been in touch with Chris before now." Again there was, not really a hesitation, a vague sense of uneasiness behind the words. Maitland waited a moment, but Foster did not seem to have anything to add, so he took himself and Conway out of the room on a note of gratitude.

VIII

"The question is, why was he so forthcoming?" said Maitland thoughtfully. They were in the Austin again, driving back towards the town; not by Cargate this time, but by a wide road that might have been its twin.

Chris might or might not have been giving the matter his full attention. He said, "Oh, I don't know," vaguely, and added after a moment, "as between one lawyer and another—"

"Come now, that's no excuse for indiscretion."

"I wouldn't have said he was particularly indiscreet."

"Perhaps not, but he just answered everything I asked him," said Antony, as though he found this frankness unreasonable. "Not that it helped at all."

"I'm beginning to wonder what you're looking for."

"Motive. Must I say it again?"

"Don't bite me. It's just that I don't see what Foster's attitude has to do with it, that's all."

"I'm sorry. I shouldn't be feeling so touchy," said Maitland, twisting round in his seat so that he could look out the back window, "if anything he had told us had been the slightest degree of use. But when you get a man who had all the virtues, and apparently none of the vices common to mankind . . . do you suppose that's why Joe killed him, because he couldn't stand the rarefied atmosphere any longer?"

"Nobody said Baker had no vices," said Chris in a matter-of-fact tone.

"No, but it was implicit . . . I say, do you realize we're being followed?"

Chris showed no signs of excitement. "There's plenty of traffic on the road."

"I know that. There was a car started up behind us when we left Foster's place, and we've made several turns, but I'm pretty sure it's the same one still there."

"When all you can see is the headlights—"

"I still think I'm right."

They were just coming up to a traffic light. "I'll turn off here," said Chris, edging the car into the near side lane. "Then we'll see."

Antony was still looking over his shoulder. "There he is," he said a moment later, the turn accomplished.

"That doesn't prove anything."

"Try the side streets, then. But don't speed up, whatever you do." A few minutes later, "He's still there," he reported.

"A coincidence, or you're imagining things," said Chris stubbornly.

"All right then, I'll have a bet with you. Go back to the hotel and draw up outside, and if a Volkswagen doesn't pass us within . . . oh, probably within thirty seconds—"

"Plenty of those about." He pulled over to the center of the road, and signaled a right-hand turn. "I suppose I'd better humor you," he added, without much expression in his voice. "What color was the car you saw in Temple Street?"

"I couldn't tell. Dark. It might have been green, or black, or even navy blue."

"The odds are still pretty heavily in your favor, wouldn't you say?"

"Scrap the bet then. But give me a chance to see if I'm right."

"Very well," said Chris, and did not speak again until he drew up a little short of the awning outside the Midland Hotel. "There!" he exclaimed, and turned to look back the way they had come. An Austin swept past, the big brother of the one they were in, and close behind came a black Volkswagen.

"I told you so," said Maitland, in a pleased tone. He had taken an old envelope out of his pocket and was scribbling on his knee.

"You really think that's been following us ever since we left Foster's house?"

"I do."

"Well, I—I'd believe you," said Chris magnanimously, "if it made any sense at all."

"It doesn't, does it?" He still sounded pleased with himself, even a little smug. "Do you think Inspector Duckett would oblige us by finding out who owns this number?" he went on, and passed over the envelope on which he had been writing.

"I daresay he'll do it for you."

"That's good. The night's still young," he added. "Come and have a drink."

"I'll have to park the car."

"If you back up a little . . . wait a bit; there's one coming out behind you."

Five minutes later they were in the smaller of the hotel's lounges and had already given their order. "Not exactly a home from home," said Antony, looking about him at the unimaginative and rather grubby beige curtains; the heavy mahogany writing desk; the unyielding chairs covered with what was undoubtedly a leather substitute; the well-trodden carpet that once, no doubt, had been a cheerful red and blue. "But at least we are alone."

"Is that so important?"

"Well, I think—"

"Look here, what have you got into your head?"

"Nothing but a thirst for knowledge." He leaned back and stretched out his legs and gave his companion a smile that was at least half-apology. "What's been going on in Arkenshaw lately?" he enquired.

"Nothing much."

"Come now, you can do better than that."

"I might, if I knew what kind of thing you mean."

"Scandal . . . crime . . . I'm really not particular."

"Well, the Lady Mayoress is suing for a divorce."

"No!"

"You needn't be sarcastic; I'm only trying to oblige," said Chris, ruffled. He was silent while the waiter came and went. "All the windows were broken one night at the

Mile End School; there have been three jewel robberies in the past year . . . more, if you take in the county area; a man whose name I forget was charged with nobbling runners at the greyhound track and a group of youths was convicted of committing a breach of the peace outside the Bishop's Move."

"That doesn't sound very hopeful."

"It's the best I can do on the spur of the moment. If you'd tell me what you're getting at—"

"Joe had a friend whom Alfred Baker disapproved of. I'm beginning to be curious, that's all."

"I don't quite see—"

"Neither do I, at this point. But it's the nearest thing to a bone of contention we've uncovered between them, isn't it?"

"Joe was up to something, and Alfred Baker found out. Is that what you think?"

"I'm beginning to wonder." He picked up his glass and looked into it as earnestly as if he were crystal gazing; then his eyes met Conway's again. "Something illegal . . . something sinful . . . with a man like Alfred Baker there's really no telling, is there?"

"I . . . see," said Chris rather blankly. He took a gulp of whisky and put the tumbler down again with a thump. "But what I don't see," he added with more assurance, "is how you think that will help."

IX

Jenny must have been waiting for his call; she answered almost as soon as the phone rang the first time. "I've been wondering," she said—perhaps she felt some explanation was necessary—"how you got on today."

"I can't really say that we progressed at all."

His mood had changed; he felt tired now, and discouraged. Jenny said carefully, "You sound—you don't sound very happy."

"I can't see why Chris wanted me to come."

"If there's really nothing you can do, you can stop worrying about it, can't you?" said Jenny reasonably. As clearly as if he were in the room with her Antony could visualize her sitting by the writing table, with the lamp-light gilding her brown curls, her gray eyes alight with interest.

He said, "That's just it, I can't be sure," almost as despondently as before, but insensibly his spirits were rising again.

"How is Arkenshaw?" Jenny wanted to know.

"Not so cold as last time I was here."

"That isn't what I meant. Is everything peaceful?"

"Quiet enough." He thought for a moment of the black Volkswagen, but after all, Chris had probably been right about that. "I don't know what you're worried about," he said, rather less than honestly.

"Uncle Nick says you set the whole town by the ears last time you were there." Sir Nicholas Harding was the head of the chambers in the Inner Temple to which Maitland belonged. If he had a fault—and his nephew would have been the first to point out that he had several—it was an inclination to plain speaking.

"Bother Uncle Nick," Antony said now, with fervor. And then, with belated caution, "Is he there?"

"No, but I had dinner with him."

"If that's his idea of cheering you up in my absence—"

"I think it was my fault, Antony. I brought the subject up."

"You should have had more sense, love. I told you, this is just an ordinary case."

"So you did," said Jenny, unrepentant. "It's funny, you know, I seem to have heard that before."

61

"There's no doubt Joe Hartley did it. There can be no harm at all in my trying to find out why."

"Can't there?" said Jenny, unconvinced. And though he spent nearly ten minutes explaining the simplicity of the situation he still seemed to detect a note of scepticism in her voice when at last they said good-night.

⋀ Saturday, 21st May

I

Maitland didn't sleep well. The bed was comfortable enough, but it creaked alarmingly whenever he turned. Chris Conway was right, of course: they might uncover Joe Hartley's motive for murder without leaving the defense in any more favorable position. And yet . . . it offended him to have to go back into court with the matter still obscure. Surely there must be some profit in knowledge, even if it were only an ability to avoid the pitfalls into which ignorance might lead. He slept at last, uneasily, and awoke, unrefreshed, to find that it was already past eight o'clock. Chris Conway had promised to call for him at nine.

He breakfasted alone, with the *Times* propped up against the coffeepot. There were premonitory rumbles from the Middlet East situation, which afterwards he was to feel, in common with half the population, had given only too adequate warning of what was to come. But that morning he gave them little attention and was no more enthralled by the information that talks with Rhodesia had been suspended or that France and Poland had signed a five-year treaty calling for cooperation in cultural, technical, and scientific matters. The problem of Joe Hartley remained stubbornly at the forefront of his mind. "It's the ingratitude that hurts," Mrs. Baker had said, and perhaps it would be fair to leave it at that . . . an act of disloyalty that could have neither justification nor excuse. He was glad that Conway's promptness did not allow him to prolong this unhelpful train of thought.

Father O'Brien, of St. Wilfred's Church, was awaiting them in his study, a comfortable room that contrived at the same time to have an impersonal air. He was a tall man with rather narrow shoulders, a thin face, and a charming smile. He had also a voice that must be an asset to any preacher, and it was when he heard him speak that Antony realized why the priest's face had seemed, from the first, so familiar.

"You must—surely you must—be related to Kevin O'Brien."

"His brother. I have heard of you from him, Mr Maitland."

That brought the familiar stab of annoyance, though surely it was unreasonable to expect that a fellow barrister, with whom he had once shared an adventure, would forever forbear from mentioning his name. It was followed closely by disappointment. "Then you haven't known the Bakers long."

"You're right, as it happens. But I don't—"

"You don't quite see the logic behind the deduction. O'Brien told me once that he had no relations in Arkenshaw now."

"I came to St. Wilfred's eighteen months ago, from a parish in Leeds." He seated himself, his chair half-turned from the desk, and gestured to his companions to take the two chairs that flanked the hearth. "But in any case I'm afraid I don't quite see how I can help you."

"I don't myself. I'm just hoping—" His gesture was vague enough to convey the insubstantial nature of his desires.

"If you mean that you are trying to find some way of

helping Joe Hartley, I should like very much to be of assistance to you."

"You knew Alfred Baker?"

"Of course." He glanced at Chris Conway and then back at Maitland again. "I can only tell you the things that everybody in Arkenshaw knows: he came regularly to Mass; he was a member of the St. Vincent de Paul Society. And then, of course, there were the children."

"When did you see him last?"

"On the day he died, at Mass . . . not to speak to."

"And before that?"

"I don't remember exactly. Probably at some time during the previous week."

"You'd remember if anything had struck you about him . . . anything unusual in his manner."

"I cannot recall anything out of the way."

"What I want to find out, you see, Father, is why Joe did it."

"Won't he tell you?"

"Not a word."

"I'm afraid I'm not a very good source of information. Joe used to be an altar boy, but he gave it up when he left school."

"Have you visited him in prison?"

"I tried to. He wouldn't see me."

That might mean anything or nothing. "Mrs. Baker wanted him to go to the seminary," Maitland said.

The priest looked startled. "Did she, indeed? It's a common enough ambition for a mother to have. Mind you, I can see why she picked on Joe. He's a quiet boy, steady—"

"That's what makes it so confusing." He caught Father O'Brien's eye, and smiled at him. "Not the most likely starter, you think?"

"If I had to guess, I'd say the younger boy, Freddie, was most likely to have a vocation."

"I see." Antony sounded thoughtful.

"I'm not implying any criticism of Joe, you know. Far from it. I have always thought of him as one of those unfortunates who end up bearing other people's burdens as well as their own."

"Whose, for instance?"

"I don't know. It was only an impression, I'm afraid. I'm probably wrong."

"Because he killed his foster father?"

"Not necessarily because of that." Again he looked from one of his companions to the other. "I find it very difficult, Mr. Maitland—"

"Yes, I can understand that." He paused, considering the wording of his next question. "You've visited the Bakers, I suppose. From those visits, did you gain any impression of dissension in the family?"

"None whatever. If you are thinking of the kind of thing that could conceivably have led to murder."

"I'm reaching the stage where I'd be glad of anything," said Antony ruefully; but the priest did not seem to have any idea of amplifying his statement. "Do you know anything about Alfred Baker's friends?"

"Mr. O'Donnell . . . Claud O'Donnell. He's one of our parishioners, and a close friend, I think. Then there is a Mr. Rawdon who made the funeral arrangements on Mrs. Baker's behalf. I had never seen him before."

"Joe's friends, then." But Father O'Brien was shaking his head.

"My own impression is that they are a self-sufficient family. I've often seen Joe with Winifred, for instance, or with that new little sister of his . . . what's the child's name? Stella. But I think perhaps if you were to ask at his school, you might get more information. He went to St. Blaise's, and I am sure Monsignor Carter would be very willing to help you."

"He promised to see us later this morning," said Chris . . .

" . . . and a fat lot of use that will be," Antony grumbled, as they left the presbytery ten minutes later. "If he's as informative as the chap we've just left—"

"What did you expect?"

"Anything . . . nothing. I hoped for some light on Joe's character, I suppose."

"I don't think, you know, that anyone's going to hand us the motive, tied up and neatly labeled," said Conway. He sounded faintly apologetic, and Antony paused with his hand on the car door to give the matter his consideration.

"Perhaps George will be able to tell us," he said at last, hopefully. "Are we going to see him?"

"Not till this afternoon; he's at work until midday." Chris had gone round to his own side of the car. "George, and Dick. Do you really want to see the little girl?"

"Stella? Of course I do."

"Well, at least . . . you won't want to see her alone," Conway said. And added defensively, when Maitland grinned at him, "I don't think it would be a good idea."

"Not *convenable*," Antony agreed. And then, "It's awkward, though, isn't it? We can't properly have either the mother or the elder sister in attendance."

"I thought of that. We can talk to her at the convent if you like."

"With one of the nuns sitting in on the interview? I suppose it's a good idea," said Maitland slowly.

"It's an excellent idea," Chris informed him with a touch of smugness. "She goes to school there, as a day girl, of course, so it'll be familiar ground."

"All right, then. Can you arrange it?"

"I can. I have. Four o'clock this afternoon."

"I see. I might have known." He got into the car and

slammed the door and added, without looking round, "Did you see that our Volkswagen's still on duty?"

"No, is it?" said Conway, repressing the impulse to look back over his shoulder and trying to get the offending vehicle into focus in the rearview mirror instead. "Are you sure it's the same one?"

"It's the same license number."

"Oh . . . well then . . . I'd forgotten about it, I'm afraid."

"Didn't you ask Inspector Duckett—?"

"I phoned him this morning, but I hadn't given another thought to it since I came out. I . . . well, I rather took it for granted—"

"That I was imagining things. I'm not, you see . . . unless you're prepared to accept the most colossal coincidence."

"No, I realize that." He started the car and drove on in silence for a while before he added, "It makes you think, doesn't it?"

"It makes you think," Maitland agreed. He wasn't at all sure that he liked the direction his thoughts were taking.

II

It was a pleasant morning, though to Antony's mind still chilly. The lilac had been out in the square when he left town, and the laburnum in old Miss Webber's backyard that he could see from the kitchen window, but so far here there was no sign of blossom. For all that, Arkenshaw had almost an air of gaiety as it basked in the spring sunshine. They were driving down Cargate now, back towards the town, and the mainstream of the traffic was headed in the same direction. The sun was warm on his left shoulder, and the passersby looked purposeful and alert. There couldn't have been a greater contrast to his own state of mind. Was any good at all going to come of the enquiries he was pursuing? It would be so easy to stop now, to continue the defense on Monday on the lines he had already laid down. If Joe Hartley had any reason, any excuse for his action, surely it was up to him to say. If any injustice was done . . . but that was something he couldn't risk, if there was any chance at all that he was wrong in his present assumption.

"If someone really is following us about," said Conway, echoing Maitland's uneasiness, "it can only mean—can't it?—that Joe has been mixed up in something shady."

"It looks like that."

Chris seemed to feel some further argument was necessary. "Whether you like it or not, your reputation is known in Arkenshaw," he said in rather an aggressive tone. "Someone is wondering what your enquiries will uncover."

"You may well be right."

"I *am* right," said Chris, becoming more positive as his companion became more vague. "The question is, is it worth going on, if all we're going to prove is that instead of being an ordinary, rather dull young man, Joe is a sort of juvenile delinquent?"

"I think we have to be sure."

"Before we discontinue our activities, you mean?"

"That's right." He turned his head and saw Chris frowning. "That's why you brought me here, after all."

"I suppose it is," said Conway grudgingly.

"The trouble with you is, you're too conscientious."

"Then that makes two of us," said Chris in a lighter tone. "Anyway, I'm still puzzled about the Bakers."

"What's bothering you?"

"Something no one is likely to tell me. I'd like to know whose fault it was—if you can call it a fault—that they had no children of their own."

"That can hardly affect the issue," said Chris dryly.

"But it's interesting . . . don't you think?"

"Not particularly."

"Oh, well!" He turned his attention to the window again. "Where are we going now?"

"To see Claud O'Donnell."

"The estate agent. Do you know him?"

"We're met over completions once or twice."

"What's he like?"

"A bit hearty. Full of goodwill."

If he had been looking for proof that Chris wasn't omniscient after all, Maitland's talk with Claud O'Donnell would have provided it. O'Donnell was a big man, somewhere in his mid-forties, at a guess; he had dark hair that waved strongly, very blue eyes, and a rather ruddy complexion. He greeted his visitors with a scowl. Any signs of goodwill were noticeably lacking.

The clerks weren't in today. The outer office was empty and surprisingly tidy. O'Donnell led them through to his own room, which was modern and colorful, with Scandinavian furniture that looked expensive. He waved a hand invitingly towards a a group of chairs, but when he sat down himself behind the desk he was still unsmiling.

"It's good of you to give us your time." That was Maitland at his most diffident, and Chris grinned to himself, knowing it was misleading; but if the intention was to placate, it wasn't very successful. If anything, the scowl intensified.

"I can't think why I agreed, and that's a fact." He looked from one of them to the other. "Unless I was curious, perhaps, to see what you'd be wanting."

"That's easily told. We want your help."

"And what are you trying to prove, then?" O'Donnell was indignant. "That young Joseph had some excuse for what he did."

"I haven't got as far as that yet. At the moment, I'd be content to know the reason."

"What reason could there be? You'll get no help from me, Mr. Maitland; I can tell you that."

Antony did not seem unduly depressed by this blunt speaking. "Tell me about Joe Hartley, then," he invited. "What do you know about him?"

"I thought he was a decent lad, but obviously I was wrong."

"I can sympathize with your attitude, but aren't you prejudging the issue?"

"You'll not be telling me he didn't do it."

"Nothing like that." He hesitated, picking his words. "If we knew his motive, it might make some difference to the way we present the case to the court."

"Boy's got a tongue in his head, hasn't he?"

"Unfortunately he won't tell us—"

"Well, then! Something he's ashamed of."

There was only too much logic about that. It echoed, besides, the fear he had admitted to Chris Conway. "I can't be sure of that," said Antony, and he wasn't surprised when O'Donnell's hand came down with a crash on the desk.

"You're making a mystery out of something that isn't mysterious at all."

"If you can enlighten me—"

"Ought to be obvious. Something Alfred found out about his conduct . . . taxed him with it . . . quarrel sprang up—"

"Something serious, then. Had Joe given any previous signs of having a murderous temper?"

"Not that I ever saw. But it happened, didn't it? Something serious enough to make him lose his head."

"Can you suggest—?"

"No, I can't." The line of questioning seemed more to his liking now; he relaxed a little, leaning back in his chair. "But I'll tell you who you ought to talk to . . . Bill Foster. Not that he'll tell you, mind. But I'd be willing to bet he could."

"Who is Bill Foster?"

"Grammar school boy. Joe's age, perhaps a little older. I'd be sorry to see any son of mine making a companion of him."

"If you could be a little more particular—"

"Bad reputation." He thought about that and turned his scowl for a moment on Chris Conway. "You'll tell me it's all rumor, I suppose. Shouldn't be surprised myself if he smoked marijuana."

Maitland frowned himself over that. "Joe shows no signs —" And again O'Donnell interrupted him.

"Bill, not Joe. But the two of them are as thick as thieves."

"I see. Do you think there was any question of pushing the drug?"

"I don't know. I'll be honest with you, Mr. Maitland, I don't know. But I've wondered, since this happened—" He broke off and smiled, not without malice. "Not what you were wanting to hear."

"Not exactly." He glanced at Chris and then back at the estate agent again. "Will you add to your kindness by telling me something about Alfred Baker?"

"That won't help you."

"I don't think it will," Maitland admitted.

"Well, then! He was a good man and a good parent. And what that meant with thirteen of them . . . I don't think I need elaborate, need I?"

"I suppose he was fond of children."

"Well, he must have been, mustn't he?" asked O'Donnell impatiently. "Though to tell you the truth I think it was a sense of duty, more than anything else. He used to say, 'somebody's got to look after them,' and he talked about a cottage in the country, when he retired and they were all grown up and self-supporting."

"I was hoping for something a little more definite. For instance, if some fault came to his notice, he wouldn't be liable to let it go unremarked?"

"If he found out what Joe was up to—"

This time it was Antony's turn to interrupt. "Forgive me, Mr. O'Donnell. We don't know yet that there was anything to find."

"I assume that because I must."

"It's an attractive theory." (The easy way out, and nobody to blame but the boy himself). "But so far it *is* only a theory."

"You'll find I'm right," O'Donnell asserted.

"Yes, perhaps. What were Mr. Baker's hobbies. How did he occupy himself in his spare time?"

For some reason this question seemed to be an infuriating one. "And why should I tell you that?"

"Bear with me," said Maitland. His smile was disarming, but it was met by an even blacker scowl.

"What use are you going to make of it?" asked O'Donnell suspiciously.

"So far as I can tell at the moment, it's for my own information only."

"And what good will it do you to know that he played chess on Mondays and Fridays and went to the St. Vincent de Paul meeting on Wednesdays, and that on the other nights he might call in for a pint at the Slubbers' Arms?"

There was a simple answer to that, but the question was probably rhetorical. "Did he play chess with you?"

"No, with Peter Rawdon. He's a clever chap, is Peter."

"I've been told that the house the Bakers live in belongs to you."

"That's right." O'Donnell was beginning to smoulder again.

"What rent do they pay?"

"What the devil has that got to do with you?"

"Nothing, I daresay. But I wish you'd tell me."

"It's nobody's business but my own."

"I was wondering, you see, about Alfred Baker's financial position."

"Poor fellow never had a ha'penny to bless himself with. Can you wonder at that?"

"It's what I should have expected," said Antony mildly. "Was there anything he was worried about?"

"If you had thirteen children—"

"Yes . . . well. I meant was there anything specific?"

"And if there was, I'd say it was his own affair, wouldn't you?"

"Certainly, but—"

"I've answered enough questions, Mr. Maitland. I'm not exactly in sympathy with your aims and objectives, you know."

"I realize that." He got up as he spoke and saw that Chris was already on his feet. "I only want to be fair to the boy," he said. It sounded like an apology, but O'Donnell's expression did not soften.

"Alfred had his point of view as well."

"I hadn't forgotten it."

"Hadn't you? You mustn't expect me to appreciate the niceties of your attitude, Mr. Maitland," said O'Donnell, and he watched stonily as they went to the door and did not return their farewells.

III

"After that," said Chris, "we'll have some coffee. Betty's is just along here."

Antony followed him along the pavement. "Why didn't you warn me?"

74

"It never ocurred to me, I'm afraid. I made the appointment with one of the clerks, and I never thought—"

"We might have expected it, I suppose. After all, I was surprised to find Foster so helpful." They were in the shop now, and Chris led the way to a table by the window. "Which reminds me, is Bill Foster his son?"

"Herbert's? Yes. Two coffees, please, and some chocolate biscuits," said Conway, who seemed for the moment to have taken charge of the expedition.

"That explains it, then."

"What does it explain?"

"Why Herbert Foster answered everything so willingly. He'd be afraid we'd ask him about his son's friendship with Joe."

"Do you really think—?"

"Every question that came along he'd answer because he was so grateful it wasn't a more difficult one."

"Yes, I daresay. But what about this drug angle? Is it what we're looking for?"

"It wants looking into, at least."

"It would explain . . . it won't help Joe though, will it?"

"There are difficulties about the theory . . . don't you think?"

"Such as?"

"We're to assume, are we, that Alfred found out what was going on (what *was* going on, anyway?) and taxed Joe with it?"

"That was what I had in mind."

"Well, where did he get his information, between lunch and tea on a Sunday afternoon, which according to the evidence he spent sleeping in his own sitting room?"

"He may not have been there all the time. He may have gone out, or someone may have called to see him."

"Without any of the children being any the wiser?"

"It doesn't sound likely."

"Still, I agree; we shall have to find out."

"It would explain the Volkswagen, wouldn't it?"

Maitland smiled at him. "You're positively leaping to conclusions, you know." There was a certain pleasing irony about the fact that he should be reproving someone else for this particular activity.

"Well, don't you think—?"

"We are now postulating a gang, to which both Joe and his friend Bill Foster belonged."

"Stranger things have happened."

"What do you know about the situation, here in Arkenshaw?"

"Not much. The *Telegraph* has run several stories, with special reference to the number of schoolchildren who are using drugs."

"Marijuana?"

"Marijuana . . . LSD . . . there was even some mention of heroin. I've no means of guessing how exaggerated the details were, of course."

"What does Dr. Conway say about it?"

"Dad? He isn't one to talk, you know. But when I mentioned the subject once to him he had his worried look."

"I see."

"And if the kids are getting hold of it, someone's selling it to them. Isn't that right?"

"We mustn't lose sight of the Volkswagen, I agree." He was stirring his coffee thoughtfully as he spoke. "Where do you suppose the driver is now?"

"In here?" said Chris, again mastering the temptation to look over his shoulder.

"He may be. Three people have come in since we did, two men and a woman. I ought to have let you sit here, where you could see the room."

"I don't think it would have occurred to me—"

76

"If you could think of something to ask the waitress, you could turn round and signal to her."

"All right. Could you eat some scones?"

"I'm always willing to sacrifice myself in a worthy cause."

"They'll be good," said Chris, seriously. He turned deliberately and raised his hand to the girl who had served them, who was standing near the kitchen door.

"The woman in the blue hat, the man with the walrus moustache, the thin-faced man in a gray suit who has hung his Burberry on the peg behind him," said Antony, his attention apparently on the street outside. The waitress came up, and Conway gave the order and turned back to his companion with a casual air so overdone that it would inevitably have given him away to anyone sitting near.

"It wouldn't be the woman, would it?" he said.

"It may not be any of them, but why not?"

"She's middle-aged."

"Not an infallible sign of innocence." He smiled again when he saw Chris frowning over this pronouncement. "You don't know any of them by sight?"

"No, I'm sorry. I don't know everyone in Arkenshaw. She looks just like anyone else," said Conway in an aggrieved tone.

"A suspicious circumstance in itself."

"If you're going to laugh—" His hurt tone reminded Maitland that in spite of his air of maturity he was still, in some ways, very young.

"Far from it. If you don't fancy the lady—and I don't myself—what about the others?"

"The man in the gray suit looks prosperous. I can't see him in a Volkswagen, can you? But then, walrus moustache doesn't look the type, either. He looks rather meek and mild, whereas I always think of Volkswagen drivers as aggressive."

"They tend to drive aggressively; that might not be the same thing."

"No," Chris agreed sadly. "We don't seem to be much further on, do we?"

"And now we need some more coffee to go with the scones," said Maitland as the waitress came up. "We shall see when we leave, I expect," he added in a consoling tone when they were alone again. "It may not be any of them."

As it turned out, the problem was easily solved. The man in the gray suit left soon after the second installment of coffee arrived, they saw him dodging the traffic to cross the road and then make off in the opposite direction from the one in which they had come; the woman in the blue hat, on the other hand, had unfolded a magazine by the time they left, and seemed to have settled down to have a good read. But walrus moustache strolled out almost on their heels, passed them on the pavement, and went straight to the Volkswagen, which was parked only a few yards behind the Austin outside the estate agent's office. "An amateur," said Maitland in a depressed tone. "An unimaginative amateur."

"Do you think so?"

"Either that, or he doesn't care if we spot him." He was silent until they were in the car again. "Where are we going now?"

"To St. Blaise's."

"Ah, yes. Monsignor—what-was-his-name?—Carter."

"He's the headmaster."

"Do you suppose—? Well, never mind. Don't try to shake off our tail, Chris. We may as well give him his money's worth."

The journey to St. Blaise's took them out of town again, this time along Market Lane and across the common that is called Moorfields. They arrived at a high stone wall, iron gates set hospitably open, an old house in spacious grounds, with a modern wing incongruously added, but half hidden behind a belt of trees.

Monsignor Carter was tall and stout, with a round, merry face and a shock of graying hair. His study was in the old part of the building, and he received them cordially, with an offer of sherry, but he was serious enough when he had got his visitors comfortably settled and turned to the business on hand.

"This is a very tragic affair."

"It is, indeed." Maitland's mood seemed to have changed, too. He seemed subdued now, a little ill at ease.

"You're trying to help Joe Hartley?" the priest asked him.

"If we can. You may be aware, Monsignor, that he absolutely refuses to give any explanation for what he did."

"His brother, Dick, told me something of the sort. I had not realized that his silence extended to his legal advisers."

"That's why we're here."

"I thought . . . a matter of a character reference, perhaps."

"You think it was out of character . . . what he did?"

"I was completely surprised when I heard of it. It made me realize how rarely we can say that, with truth."

"Have you seen him in prison, Monsignor?"

"I should have liked to, of course, but he has been stubbornly opposed to the idea. I understand Father O'Brien, even, met with the same rebuff."

"You yourself can think of no reason—?"

"None at all. But you must remember that I have seen very little of Joe since he left school."

"How well did you know Alfred Baker?"

"Hardly at all. He might attend the Sports, or on Speech Day. I knew of him, of course."

"Have all the boys been to St. Blaise's?"

"George and Joe and Fred. Dick is still with us. I believe the next one is Michael, who will be coming in two or three years."

"All on scholarships?"

The question seemed to startle Monsignor Carter. Perhaps it was an unexpected one. "When Mr. and Mrs. Baker were making so many sacrifices to give the children a good start in life it seemed the least we could do," he said, after a little hesitation.

"I see. Tell me about Joe, then. If I asked you to give me an appraisal of his character, what would you say?"

"Not a brilliant boy. Rather a plodder, really."

"Yes, but did he get where he wanted in the end?"

That, too, required some thought. "I think he did. I was sorry, at any rate, that he did not stay to take his 'A' levels, but I could quite understand his anxiety to be earning his living, you know."

"It was his own idea?"

"So far as I know."

"Would you say Joe was fond of money?" His attention might have been completely taken up by the play of light on the glass at his elbow.

"I don't think I can answer that question. I haven't any knowledge on which to base an assumption."

"How was his temper?"

"Equable, on the whole." He hesitated again. "There were one or two incidents—"

"Please tell me." He said that quickly, even with a sort of eagerness, and the priest gave him a rather rueful smile.

"They weren't really illuminating, I'm afraid. Just rather out of character."

"Even so—"

"Nothing very out of the way. I don't suppose we shall ever eliminate fighting, altogether."

"So Joe's a fighter, is he?" (He isn't fighting now.)

80

"On at least two occasions . . . two occasions that came to my notice, I should say. Each time it seemed that Joe had been the aggressor . . . at least, he made no attempt to deny the fact. But I can't say that in either case I really got to the bottom of the affair."

"You mean he wouldn't tell you? That's exactly what's happening now."

"Except that it is rather more serious."

"Of course it is. But the analogy is there. Who would know why Joe got into those two fights, do you suppose?"

His sudden enthusiasm seemed to bewilder the priest. "Certainly not the masters who separated them: Mr. Dawson in one instance, Mr. Hastings in the other. They were as much in the dark as I was."

"The boys he was fighting with—presumably they knew why."

"If they remember. I can't imagine it was anything very important."

"You said it was out of character. Don't tell me you've forgotten who else was involved."

"I remember on the second occasion it was a boy called Keating."

"How long ago was this?"

"Two years, more or less."

"Is Keating still at school?"

"He'll be leaving us in July. His father's a chemist. He has a shop in Cargate, not far from St. Wilfred's."

"Thank you. What about Joe's friends?"

"Two who come to mind are Illingworth and Carter . . . no relation of mine." He saw that Chris had his notebook out and paused to give him the addresses. "They left at the same time that Joe did. I can't say whether their friendship persisted, of course."

"You don't think . . . have you had any trouble with drugs?"

81

"There have been cases. I think there are not many schools nowadays who would not have to admit as much as that. If you're asking me whether Joe took drugs, I can answer very positively, no. He was far too keen on sports to do anything—"

"Pep pills?"

"No. I think I know him well enough to say that."

"But you would have said—wouldn't you?—that he was equally unlikely to commit murder."

"Yes, I'm afraid . . . yes, I should have said that. But I still don't feel . . . do you think Joe is taking drugs now?"

"No. But it has been suggested that a friend of his—a grammar school boy, Monsignor, not one of yours—is on marijuana, and if there is any truth in the allegation, I should like to know."

"I can give you no information about that."

"Do you think Joe is honest?"

This time there was no hesitation. "Oh, yes. I have always thought him completely straightforward."

"Not likely, then, to engage in drug-trafficking."

"My dear Mr. Maitland, the boy is only seventeen!"

"That does not entirely preclude the possibility. Someone distributes the stuff, after all."

"What I know of him—" He broke off and added after a pause, despondently, "You are going to remind me again that I didn't know him very well."

"It is said that murder is the one crime that anyone might commit."

"That is something beyond my experience, I am afraid."

"Yes, of course," said Maitland meaninglessly, and drank the last of his sherry. "I'm grateful for your time, Monsignor, and more than grateful for what you have told us."

"A very little, I'm afraid."

"No . . . I don't know. Do you believe in retribution, Monsignor?"

"Are you asking me that as a schoolmaster or as a priest?"

"Not, I think, as a schoolmaster." But he went on, without waiting for a reply, "*Revenge is a kind of wild justice, which the more man's nature runs to, the more ought law to weed it out.*"

"I don't think I quite understand you, Mr. Maitland."

"Joe's going to prison for what he did. I don't want him to spend any longer there than—than he deserves."

"Surely that is a matter for the judge, and the jury."

"Finally, yes. That doesn't abrogate my own responsibility."

"Even if . . . in the course of our conversation you have hinted at some very disagreeable possibilities."

"Possibilities . . . probabilities. I'd give something to be able to understand Joe Hartley."

"I'm sorry to see you so worried—"

"Thank you, Monsignor."

"—but I'm sure you'll do your best," said the priest, meaning well, and did not understand why Maitland's answering smile grew suddenly so bleak.

IV

They did some cross-country work after they left the school, and Maitland, who had been beginning to feel he was getting to know Arkenshaw, was completely lost again. Chris drew up at length outside a long, stone building with neat flower beds under lattice windows and a weathered sign on which the words "Slubbers' Arms" could faintly be made out. Antony was out on the pavement and studying it when Chris came round the car to join him. "I can't make anything of the illustration," he said.

"Nothing very interesting. A man in a brat."

"In a what?"

"You ignorant southerners! A sort of warehouse coat I suppose you'd call it."

"I'll call it anything you like. Now why have I always imagined the Slubbers' Arms to be an unattractive place, if not actually squalid?"

"I can't think."

"The name is not exactly poetic; I daresay that's the reason. Will they give us bread and cheese?"

"They will. And some good draft beer. What is more to the point, I've arranged to meet Inspector Duckett here."

"You think of everything. Of course, we must be quite near Old Peel Farm."

"Not more than a quarter of a mile away." He turned his head as the black Volkswagen pulled into the car park. "There's our friend again. Shall I ask him what he wants?"

"No good. He'd only express polite bewilderment, and you'd lose your temper."

"I don't often do that."

"I really can't see what else there would be to do."

Fred Duckett was awaiting them in the bar and had commandeered a corner table for their use. Antony was getting used to seeing him out of uniform now. Chris went to the bar to give their order, and Maitland took a seat with his back to the window.

"And what, may I ask, are you getting into now, Mr. Maitland?" said the inspector by way of greeting, in an admonitory tone.

Antony smiled at him vaguely. "You're going to tell me, aren't you? I suppose you mean you've found out who the car belongs to."

"I have that." He let the silence lengthen and kept his eyes on Chris until his son-in-law came across to the table to join them, bringing first a couple of tankards and then going back again for two plates of new bread and what the barmaid assured him was "a bit of real Wensleydale."

"It belongs to a man called Fennister," the inspector said then. "Harry Fennister," he repeated, and looked from one of his companions to the other, as though expecting to observe some sign of emotion.

"Never heard of him," said Chris.

"Well, I daresay you wouldn't have, at that."

"Who is he?"

"Petty crook."

"I see," said Maitland thoughtfully. "Or rather," he corrected himself, "I don't. What, exactly, is his line?"

"Sneak thief," said Duckett, who seemed in a taciturn mood.

"Who are his associates?"

"A chap known as Simple Simon . . . not that Harry's all that bright himself. And Teddy Hill, who does odd jobs at the greyhound track and a bit of pickpocketing on the side."

"I don't see," said Chris, frowning into his beer, "how that fits in."

"Nor me, neither."

"Does Fennister have a walrus moustache?" Maitland asked and turned to survey the room.

"He had last time I saw him," said the inspector, not committing himself.

"He hasn't come in. Unless there's another bar."

"There isn't."

"All right, then. I expect he's waiting in the car. Might he be running errands for someone in—in a bigger way of business?"

"For one of the mobs, do you mean? I'd say it was very likely."

"Who, for instance?"

"That I can't tell you." He bit into his sandwich and chomped silently for a while. "It's a reet puzzle, lad, and that's a fact."

"Let's see if we can come to it another way, then. What do you know of a boy called Bill Foster? A grammar school boy, I believe."

"Nothing good," said the inspector darkly.

"Well, but . . . what precisely?"

"Nothing precisely." Duckett sounded slightly indignant, as though the question was an unreasonable one. "He hangs around t' Peppermint Stick which is enough to damn him in itself."

"Why?"

"It's a sort of teen-age club."

"Sounds innocent enough."

"That's all you know. Sithee, lad," said Fred Duckett, all at once very much in earnest, "there's suspicion, and there's proof. As sure as I'm sitting here they're pushing drugs, and one of these days we'll catch them at it."

"And is Bill Foster—er—exploiter or victim?"

"Both, if you ask me."

"I see," said Antony again. And then, more briskly, "Did Joe Hartley also frequent this place?"

"He's been there," admitted Duckett grudgingly. "I'd have said his hands were clean."

"Until the murder, you mean?"

"Aye. It would explain, wouldn't it, what Alfred was on at him about?"

"It would." It occurred to him then that if the inspector had been less closemouthed, if he had confided his suspicions to Chris Conway, the present situation wouldn't have arisen. Conway wouldn't have briefed him, and they wouldn't be sitting here, the three of them . . . "Your Dr. Naylor would have told you, wouldn't he, Chris, if Joe was on drugs himself?"

"Of course."

"That doesn't clear him, though, of the other possibility. I've been told there's a problem in the town, Inspector. What do you know of the source of supply?"

"We know t' organization's there; we haven't come near it," said Duckett heavily. "We've picked up a few of the small fry, of course. Nothing to signify."

"Young people among them?"

"A couple of eighteen-year-olds. Yes."

"Do you know anything to connect Harry Fennister with the drug traffic?"

"Not a thing. Mind you, I'd not say it was unlikely."

"What else is going on in Arkenshaw that is as worrying as the drugs?"

"While t' foreigners are here," said the inspector dourly, "there'll always be trouble."

"Nothing to do with the Pakistani population; at least I don't think so."

"What are you getting at?"

"I'm fishing in the dark. Not a profitable occupation. Chris mentioned something about jewel robberies."

"He did, did he? I'd say that was a problem to t' whole of Thorburndale, not just to Arkenshaw."

"Well, what else has been going on? What do your colleagues in the detective branch talk about when they let down their back hair?"

Duckett looked questioningly at his son-in-law, but Chris only shook his head and gave him a blank look. "I don't see what you're at, Mr. Maitland," said the inspector in a tone of discontent. "There's been some fires . . . suspicion of arson. Investigation's going on now, along with t' insurance people."

"Private houses? Business premises?"

"One office building and a couple of warehouses. It's nowt to do wi' Joe Hartley, all this."

"Or with our friend the Walrus?"

"Not as I knows on."

"No, I see." He pulled his plate towards him and cut himself a piece of cheese. "There doesn't seem to be much else to say, does there? Who lives may learn."

"You'll take care," said the inspector, glaring at him with almost as much animosity as old Mrs. Duckett might have shown in similiar circumstances. "Both of you," he added, and Maitland looked up and smiled at him disarmingly.

"We'll take care," he promised. "Is Harry so dangerous?"

"I'd say he's mean-minded. Spiteful," said Fred Duckett, diving to the bottom of his vocabulary and coming up with the *mot juste*.

"But not efficient."

"No." He sounded doubtful, and for a moment Antony thought he was going to add something to the admission. But then he clamped his lips together tightly, picked up his tankard, and got up and made for the bar. When he came back he said in a thoughtful way, "I think I'll just have a word with Harry, when we leave."

But when they went out to the car park twenty minutes later neither the Volkswagen nor its driver was anywhere to be seen.

V

The Slubbers' Arms is in Fairfield Road, which was quiet at that time of day. When the lights changed, Chris negotiated the turn into Cargate with his usual caution and tucked himself in behind a builder's truck which was following a tramcar down the hill towards the center of the town. He seemed to be absorbed in his own thoughts, and Maitland did not try to interrupt him. He had plenty to think about himself.

But instead of proceeding in any useful direction, his

mind would persist in dwelling on Inspector Duckett, and it wasn't very far from him to Grandma, and he began to wonder, as he had wondered before in the night watches, whether he had made the most of his opportunities in that direction. Grandma wasn't one, as she would no doubt have told him roundly, to push herself in where she wasn't wanted, but perhaps with a bit of encouragement . . .

It was at this point in his meditations that he realized something was wrong.

Chris was lying well behind the lorry, so there should have been no difficulty at all when it braked rather suddenly to a standstill opposite the turning into Cunliffe Road. If he reacted quickly, that should have been all to the good. He slammed down the brake, and nothing whatever happened, except that they swerved violently to the right and found themselves facing the bonnet of an XKE Jaguar, which was dawdling up the hill at a decorous thirty. There was nothing for it but to try to make the gap between truck and car, which looked impossibly narrow. The Jaguar's driver accelerated, in an attempt to get round the corner into Cunliffe Road, using it as an escape route. Chris had his foot on the floorboards, but still the brakes didn't respond. The two cars met with a sickening crash in the middle of the intersection and came to a standstill, locked, as it were, in mortal combat, the crumpled front wing of the Austin entwined in the crumpled rear wing of the Jaguar.

There followed a moment of stunned silence, while the parties concerned realized that they were still alive. Chris was trying to wind his window down, but without success; he followed Maitland out into the road, stalked past him without a word, without even pausing to view the damage, and went round to the near side of the Jaguar to confront the driver when he scrambled over the passenger seat and emerged.

"You!" he said unfairly. "What the bloody hell did you think you were doing?"

The Jaguar's driver pointed out, not in a spirit of mildness, that he, at least, was on his own side of the road.

"You could have stopped—"

"And waited for you to crash into me."

"I suppose you'll tell me you meant well."

"I nearly made it. If I could have got into that side street—"

"But you couldn't, could you?"

"What's the odds? We might have met head on . . . I suppose that would have suited you better."

Chris, still heatedly, asked him what he meant.

The lorry driver had pulled his vehicle into the side of the road and come over to join them. He stood a moment, eyeing the two contestants in a tolerant way, winked at Antony, said, "You were lucky, mate," and lay down on his back and began to edge his way under the Austin, pausing to add, before he disappeared altogether, "These little old ladies. Right out in front of me she walks, waving an umbrella. Well, I asks you, mate, what was I to do?"

A small crowd had gathered on the pavement by this time, the traffic was beginning to pile up on both sides of the road, and, rather to Maitland's relief, a policeman was making his way towards them with the long strides of a man who covers the ground at speed without ever seeming to be in a hurry. The two drivers looked as if they would be quite content to continue their slanging match all the afternoon, but they both turned on the constable when he came up, each demanding his attention and sympathy for his own point of view. Maitland judged the time might have come when intervention would prove profitable and laid a restraining hand on Conway's arm. He thought afterwards that it was difficult to see how the situation would have resolved itself if the lorry driver hadn't chosen that moment to emerge again, a little oilier than before, but still good-humored, and addressed himself to Chris.

"You want to be careful the sort of friends you make, young man. There's someone been monkeying with your brakes."

Chris calmed down a little after that and applied himself to clearing up the formalities with as little delay as possible. Inspector Duckett was not to be found, but the use of his name expedited matters somewhat. Conway even made his peace with the owner of the Jaguar, which Antony had privately considered an impossible task, as he turned out to be a rally driver who regarded both his skill and his car as sacrosanct. When at last they were free to go, and had watched the two cars being towed ignominiously away, Conway turned to Maitland and said rather blankly, "What now?"

"We want a hire car. Not a self-drive."

"Don't you trust yourself with me?"

"Don't be an idiot. I want to make sure nothing else happens." He paused, expectantly, but added when Chris was silent, "It has occurred to you, of course, that this was Harry's idea of a joke."

"Of course, but—"

"If we get a car with a driver, he can at least make sure that the same thing doesn't happen again."

"All right, then. If we can find a telephone—"

"There's one on the corner behind you." They began to move towards it. "I'm sorry about all this, you know."

"The insurance will take care of it," said Chris in a depressed tone.

"You'll have some interesting bruises, I'm afraid."

"We both shall, I imagine. It's lucky it was no worse." They reached the telephone box. "I'll tell them we want one with a division between driver and passengers, shall I? Then we can talk if we want to."

This seemed to Maitland to be an excellent idea.

VI

The Bakers' house was large and untidy, and a large and untidy garden straggled round it. They arrived there, of course, much later than they had expected, but George must have been on the lookout for them; he had the door open before they had time to ring. The hall was square, with a tiled floor and some spurious paneling. "We can talk in the dining room," said George. "Or we can go into the sitting room if you'd rather."

"The sitting room, unless you've any objection."

"Me? No; why should I?" His laugh sounded false to Maitland's ears, but was probably only intended to show his unconcern. At nineteen, anything to do with sentiment was most likely at a discount.

He led the way, and Conway and Maitland followed him into a room at the left of the hall. The house was oddly silent. It was a big room, rather shabby, but undeniably comfortable. Tall windows opposite the door looked out on a tangle of shrubbery; a smaller window in the wall opposite the fireplace faced the street. "It was over there," said George, gesturing towards the hearth rug, which looked like a new one. He seemed both fascinated by the crime and embarrassed, which Antony thought in the circumstances a reasonable enough state of mind.

He was a tall young man, with dark hair that was far too long, and the kind of good looks that wouldn't have shamed a film star. In addition, he was much too neatly dressed. Antony regarded him with some amusement and was further amused to see that Chris Conway was irritated by the boy's appearance and his affectations. Arthur Augustus D'Arcy, thought Maitland, and caught himself up on the verge of smiling. George wouldn't have seen the joke, and in any case had probably never even heard of the *Magnet*. "I'm very glad to talk to you, of course," he was saying now with a faintly worried air, "but I can't see how anyone can do anything to help." He hesitated. "I mean, Joe did it, didn't he, and how are you going to get round that?"

On the whole that seemed like a question it was as well to leave unanswered. Antony glanced again at Conway, who still had that faintly ruffled air. "Mr. Maitland has one or two questions to ask you," said Chris, as if George hadn't spoken. "We shan't keep you long."

"No . . . of course . . . we should sit down, shouldn't we?" He was trying very hard to sound in command of the situation, but his uneasiness betrayed itself with every word. "Over here," he said, and indicated a group of chairs near the window. "We shan't be disturbed. Mum's lying down, and Win took the little ones out."

"It's no good our asking you about the day it happened, is it?" said Antony, settling himself in a large armchair with a torn and rather grubby chintz cover. "You were out the whole afternoon?"

"Yes; I went out straight after dinner and didn't get home until seven o'clock in the evening," said George. It was hard to tell whether he was relieved to say this or very faintly regretful.

"But we can ask you to tell us a little about your foster father. Did he seem on good terms with Joe when they met at the dinner table?"

"He was asking questions . . . of all of us, not just of Joe. He seemed in quite a good mood, and Joe didn't say anything to upset him."

"They were generally on good terms?"

"Nothing out of the way."

Maitland smiled at him. "What does that mean?"

"Well . . . Dad was a bit old-fashioned, you know." He gave the impression that he was picking his words carefully; his own vocabulary, perhaps, would have been beyond their understanding.

"You're telling me there were things about Joe that he didn't approve of."

"He thought Joe was a bit too keen on sports, as a matter of fact."

"That doesn't sound very serious."

"You asked me—"

"Yes, but I think you could make the matter clearer, if you would." When George did not answer he added, quietly insistent, "Joe had a friend called Bill Foster."

"If you know all about it, I don't see why you want to ask me," said George. He sounded sulky now. The artificial manner didn't go very deep.

"I need confirmation of what I've heard. You know Bill yourself, I suppose."

"I've known him all my life."

"Well then! You can tell me—"

"He isn't a bad sort of chap. A bit brainy, actually . . . not Joe's type, I should have thought."

"Did you approve of the connection?"

"It wasn't up to me."

"You're entitled to an opinion."

"Yes . . . well . . . Dad didn't like it. He'd heard things about Bill."

"What, for instance?"

"That he was on pot."

"Do you think that's true?"

"I've heard him talk that wildly you'd think he was daft," said George, his North Country accent suddenly very strong.

"I see."

"I don't know anything about drugs myself," said George, as belligerently as though he didn't expect to be believed.

"All right; let's go back to Joe again. Would you say he was easily led?"

"Anything but. A stubborner chap if he made up his mind to a thing—" He let the sentence trail, but his look was expressive. He seemed relieved to have left a difficult subject behind.

"We've heard no mention of girl friends."

George laughed. "Tell you the truth," he said confidentially, "I don't think he was all that interested. He was just as happy taking Stella for a walk, or Win to a church social." His tone had all the scorn of a practiced man of the world.

"That couldn't have been the cause of the quarrel, then."

"Did they quarrel?"

"Why do *you* think Joe killed your foster father?"

The direct question seemed to take George aback. He muttered, "I haven't the faintest idea," and then added in a troubled way, "I thought he just went off his head, you know."

"Had he shown any previous signs of insanity?"

"No. I just thought it must have been that way."

"Did Mr. Baker do the Football Pools?"

George seemed not so much surprised as relieved by the abrupt change of direction. "No," he said, quoting. "He thought it was an activity for little minds."

"Does that apply to other forms of gambling, too?"

"I'd say he just wasn't interested." He came to his feet as Maitland did, and added, for good measure, "He was very keen on chess."

"So I've heard. Is Dick at home? You know I want to talk to him as well."

"I'll fetch him." But he went first to the front window and pulled aside the lace curtain. "What sort of a car do you drive, Mr. Conway? It's an Austin Princess, isn't it? Do you like it?"

"It's a hire car, I don't know what it's like to drive."

"Oh—?"

"Mine's an 1100. It suits me very well, but it's being repaired at the moment."

"What a bore. What do you drive, Mr. Maitland?"

He hadn't driven for so long he very rarely thought of the reason, but he didn't need the question to remind him that his shoulder was aching abominably after the shaking up he had received that afternoon. "We have a Jaguar," he said, and thought for a moment of Jenny, her hands firm on the wheel, and how she contrived to be at once relaxed and completely absorbed by what she was doing. If she'd been driving the XKE . . .

"How splendid!" There was genuine enthusiasm there, but still Maitland had the impression that the word had been carefully chosen.

"Not a very new one," he said apologetically, but George seemed unimpressed by this and went away happier, apparently, than he had been at any time since the interview began.

VII

The list of the Baker's foster children was even more tattered now. A hasty consultation reminded Antony that Dick was twelve years old. He was a fair, rather pale boy, slightly built, with a lively air about him that might have been nervous in origin, or that might have been the result of a superabundance of physical energy. He was more obviously upset than George had been, and he started talking almost at once when Conway had introduced himself and his companion. "It's dreadful about Dad. I can't think what got into Joe. He's a good sort, you know . . . I've always thought he was a good sort. Not excitable."

"We're puzzled, too," said Conway, much more at his ease with the younger boy. "That's why I thought you might be able to help us."

Dick seemed to be following his own train of thought. "They don't hang people now, do they? Freddie said they didn't. But I don't think being in prison for life is much of a catch. Joe wouldn't like it."

That I can believe, Maitland thought, and suddenly wished that the interview was over and they were out in the open again. The room wasn't over warm; he couldn't have told why he found it suddenly so oppressive. He said aloud, "It may not be as bad as that," and did not think until later that a life sentence probably meant to Dick exactly what it said, no less.

"Well, I hope not. I know when you do a thing you have to—to take the consequences," said Dick seriously. "But it wasn't like Joe at all, you know . . . what he did."

"Hasn't he a temper?"

"Oh, yes, but it takes some rousing. And then—" He stopped, and his eyes went sideways, as though he were trying to see without actually turning his head the place where Alfred Baker had fallen.

"You have already implied that you can think of no reason—"

"No, I can't."

"You were with him that morning?"

"Yes, but we weren't talking. We were in the back garden, and he was bowling to me. He's pretty good at cricket; it's a pity he gave it up."

"Don't you think you'd have been able to tell if anything had happened to upset him?"

"I suppose it would have been obvious." Dick thought

about that for a moment. "I'm sure it would," he added positively.

"And at dinner time?"

"There was nothing wrong, except that George gets riled if you ask him where he's going."

"No trouble between Joe and Mr. Baker?"

"No."

"Tell me about the afternoon, then. You stayed at home?"

"Yes, I'd promised Joe I'd help dry the pots. It didn't really take so very long."

"And then?"

"I went into the playroom with a book."

"Where was Mr. Baker?"

"In here."

"Do you know if he went out at all during the afternoon or if anyone came to see him?"

"He wouldn't be likely to go out once he'd settled down for a nap."

"Would you have heard if he had done so?"

"No, I suppose I wouldn't. The telly was on most of the time, and Freddie isn't ever exactly quiet, and all the kids were there, so there was a good deal of shouting and carrying on."

"I see." He wondered how much of Dick's attention had actually been concentrated on the book he was reading. "And if anybody came to the house?"

"Win would have heard the bell. She was in the kitchen all the time."

"Unless someone came round to one of the windows of this room, and attracted Mr. Baker's attention that way."

"Why should they do that?"

"I don't know. But if they had done it, and Mr. Baker had gone himself to let them in—"

"It sounds a pretty daft setup, but I suppose it could have happened."

"Thank you." He hesitated a moment, and then came to his feet. "Do you know, I think that is all I want to ask you."

"And now you're going to talk to Stella."

"I hope so. Is she—?"

"She's gone up to the convent. You won't get anything out of her, you know. A kid like that!"

"Why not?"

"Ever since it happened she does nothing but cry."

"*All* the time?"

"Of course not." Dick was impatient with this literal interpretation of his statement. "But she hasn't a word for anyone, you know. Just creeps about looking miserable."

It didn't sound exactly encouraging. "And as for Joe," Maitland said, as they went out to the car a few minutes later, "he grows more and more of a puzzle."

"What's on your mind?"

"George's statement. Do you remember what you were like at seventeen?"

"Well, I never had a sister, but if I had, I don't think I'd have been taking her out, if that's what you mean."

"Kevin O'Brien told me something of the horror of church socials in Arkenshaw. They sing 'Come back to Erin,' and probably 'The mountains o' Mourne.' I don't exactly remember."

"They may have changed for the better since then," said Chris, giving the matter his earnest attention.

"So I should hope. But you see what I mean, don't you?"

"Perhaps Joe repressed all his natural instincts until he had to break out somewhere."

"Now we're back with psychology again. We'll have enough of that on Monday . . . don't you think?" Antony got into the car and shut the door with an air of finality. "Do you think you dare speak to Claud O'Donnell again."

"I'll chance it if you really want me to."

"A telephone call would do. I never asked him when he saw Alfred Baker last."

"If he'd been the one to tip him off about something Joe did, he'd have told us."

"So I think." He sounded depressed. "All the same, I should like to know."

VIII

In spite of the contempt Dick expressed for her youth, it seemed that Stella was a year older than he was. Maitland stuffed the list back into his pocket and said gloomily, "It doesn't sound very hopeful, does it?"

They were standing together at the top of the six steps that led up to the convent door, and Conway had just pulled the bell. They could hear it jangling somewhere deep inside the building. Chris turned now to look at his companion and said, frowning, "What are you hoping for?"

"If Alfred Baker saw no one during the afternoon, something must have happened to Joe while he was out."

"And you think the child can tell us?"

"Unless he left her at any time during their walk. And even that might be illuminating."

The door opened then, and Chris turned to speak to the girl who had opened it: a dark girl with a bad complexion, and wearing a very ugly black frock. "I think Sister Mary Dominic is expecting us."

"Sister said to put you in the parlor." Her voice was more attractive than her appearance, with a hint of brogue, as though she hadn't, perhaps, been very long in Arkenshaw. She led the way across the hall, so highly polished that Antony found himself treading warily, to a door on the left with the words "Saint Peter" printed in poker work on a varnished board above it.

The parlor was a stiff, uncomfortable room whose chairs, far from accepting you into a comfortable embrace, were obviously never intended to have more than a nodding acquaintance with the people who used them. The seats were upholstered in satin, black and cream stripes, and the curtains matched them, and the general effect was depressing in the extreme. Maitland prowled across to the window and pulled back the net curtain, and he stood looking out on a wide lawn and the trees beyond just hazing into leaf. He was thinking about the girl who had admitted them and wondering if she found a refuge here from a world that is not always kind; and then the door opened and shut again with a decisive click, and he turned to see a tall woman who had obviously never needed a refuge of any kind, unless perhaps . . .

His thoughts drifted off into incoherence. The black and white of her habit suited her, even the headdress, ugly in itself, seemed to make a charming frame for a beauty of the classical type that is all too rarely seen. Later, he could have told you that she was too pale, that her eyebrows were a little too heavy for her face; but immediately he was aware of a humorous look, of gray eyes that seemed to take a great deal of pleasure in the world around her. Searching for words, he decided that he found in her a sort of steady contentment.

Chris had already effected the introductions. She looked at him for a moment and then at Antony, dividing her words between them. "I thought I should like to speak to you before I brought Stella in."

"It's kind of you to help us out."

"No, Mr. Conway . . . the least I can do." Her eyes turned to Maitland then, finding him perhaps the more formidable of the two. "I needn't ask you to be gentle with her. She's a very nervous child."

"I'm sorry to hear that," said Antony, and perhaps at that moment his sympathy was more for himself than for Stella. Sister Mary Dominic must have realized this, for she smiled at him and said quickly,

"I know it's difficult, but I do assure you . . . with most girls you'd have quite a different problem. Too brash, too self-confident. Stella's not like that. Of course, the Bakers are kindness itself, but she's only been with them two years."

"I see." He thought he did, and he didn't find the outlook encouraging. "I'll be careful," he promised. And then, "Has she spoken to you at all about what happened?"

"She didn't come to school for a week afterwards. Winnie came to tell me why. When Stella did come back the least thing upset her; it seemed best not to worry her with questions."

"Then, when I bring up the subject now—"

"I quite realize that you feel you have no alternative. She is not without courage, you know, and I have tried to make her understand—" She paused there and said after a moment, "Shall I bring her in now."

"Just a moment. I suppose you don't know Joe."

"Oh, but I do. He's an Old Boy."

"I didn't think—"

"He was in the kindergarten here."

"That's a long time ago."

"I wonder if he has changed so much. You're worried about Joe, aren't you, Mr. Maitland?"

"Very worried."

"Well . . . he was a stubborn little boy." She smiled, taking him into her confidence. "He did not, of course, know the phrase 'it's a matter of principle,' but if he had done, that's what he'd have said."

"I see." He added, half to himself, "There is still Alfred Baker's point of view."

"Yes, of course," she agreed quickly. But if she felt any partisanship, she wasn't going to explain or excuse it. "Shall I fetch Stella now?"

"Please do." It would have been easier, he thought, to have seen the child alone, to have had no witnesses if he treated her clumsily, as he felt inevitably would be the case. Sister Mary Dominic smiled at him again, the encouraging sort of smile she might have given to a backward pupil, and went out of the room. Stella couldn't have been far away, because the nun was back in a moment, shepherding the girl in front of her.

After what Dick had said, Antony was glad that she wasn't actually crying, though her eyelids were swollen, and it seemed likely that some tears had been shed not long before. Stella was small and slightly built, with dark, silky hair, gray eyes, a short, straight nose, and a tremulous mouth. Taken all in all, enchantingly pretty, in a way the newspaper picture hadn't shown, but he thought she looked even younger than her thirteen years. If she was calm, it was with a sort of frozen calmness; Antony wondered again if it was her foster father's death or Joe Hartley's predicament that affected her most.

"This is Stella," Sister Mary Dominic was saying. "Mr. Conway, Stella, and Mr. Maitland, who wants to ask you some questions."

They were both on their feet. "Will you come and sit over here, Stella?" She went obediently to the chair he had indicated. This time Sister Mary Dominic sat down on a small sofa, a little removed from her three companions. She seemed to have achieved a fair degree of detachment, but when Maitland glanced at her a few moments later her eyes were fixed anxiously on Stella's face. "Nothing very terrible," he said, speaking to the girl again. "We shan't even keep you very long."

She said, "No," not much above a whisper.

"You can guess what I want to ask you about, I expect."

She did not answer straightaway, but then she said tentatively, "About the day Mr. Baker . . . died."

"Yes, I'm afraid so. But tell me something about yourself first."

She seemed to shrink away from the question. "I don't . . . there's nothing to tell."

He didn't really think that anything he could say would reassure her. "Well, for instance . . . how long have you been coming here to school?"

"Two years." She paused there, but when it became evident he wasn't going to speak again she added desperately, "Mum brought me when I first came to live with them."

"With the Bakers?"

"Yes." This time the hesitation was shorter. "My own parents were killed, you see, in an air crash." She made the statement flatly, with no apparent emotion.

"I'm sorry. That was bad luck, wasn't it?"

"Oh, it was." It was no more than a polite agreement. For the first time he began to wonder whether this stiffness was actually better than tears would have been. If he could only get her to relax . . .

"Have you any brothers and sisters?"

"Not of my own."

"And now you have twelve."

"Five sisters and seven brothers. If you count Joe."

"Don't you want to count him?"

"I don't know. You see . . . nobody ever mentions him now."

"Where did you live, until two years ago?"

"At the other side of Arkenshaw. Out on the Stavethorpe Road."

"So you didn't know the Bakers before. Or any of your new family."

"No."

"How did it feel, suddenly to become one of a crowd?"

He hadn't thought she could go any further away from him, but now he sensed her withdrawal. "It felt . . . very strange," she said. He thought there was bewilderment behind the words.

"Tell me about it," he suggested.

"Mum is very good to me," she said quickly, as though he had disputed the fact.

"I'm sure she is. What about your foster father?"

She bit her lip. "Mr. Baker was kind. Very kind." For the first time there was some warmth in her voice. "And patient," she added.

He smiled at her then. "Do you need people to be patient with you?" But she looked back at him without any change of expression.

"I'm very stupid sometimes." The warmth had gone now, she sounded as though the thought made her angry.

"In what way?"

"I don't know. Forgetful. *Stupid*," she said again.

"I see. What about the rest of the family?" When she was silent he added, questioningly, "George?"

"George is grown up," she said, dismissing him. "So is Winnie, really . . . she has a job . . . I think she must be clever, but she doesn't make you feel it."

"Do you help her with the housework?"

"I try to." For the first time he thought she forgot Sister Mary Dominic's presence and spoke to him almost naturally. "I expect I ought to try harder."

"Why?"

"Because—" (she hadn't forgotten the nun after all)

"—I ought to be grateful for having a good home. If it weren't for Mum, I might be in an orphanage."

"Would that be so dreadful?" he asked, answering the tone rather than the words.

"They aren't always . . . kind."

"Who told you that?"

"Freddie."

"He was teasing you."

"That's what he always says. I was *only teasing.*" She looked forlorn again. "I don't understand him most of the time," she said.

"I shouldn't let that worry you."

"No," she agreed doubtfully.

"What about the rest of them?"

"Dick's mad about cricket. We don't have much in common, really," she said with a sudden, odd effect of primness. "And the others are just babies, you know."

"You haven't mentioned Joe."

"No," she said, and looked past him, out of the window, and then down at her hands; anywhere, so that she did not meet his eyes. "Will they keep him in prison?"

How was he to answer that? He didn't even know what answer she wanted to hear. She might be anxious about Joe; she might even be frightened of him; there was no way to tell. "I don't think you must expect anything else," he told her.

"All his life?"

"Not as long as that, Stella. I'm afraid I can't tell you how long." At her age, a year must seem an eternity. He waited, but she made no attempt to speak again, and after a while he continued, "You went walking with him . . . that day."

"I like walking."

"Did you often go with Joe?"

"Yes, quite often."

"I suppose he was . . . kind to you, too," he said, suddenly impatient with the word. Something in his tone brought Stella's eyes to meet his own again.

"I don't know. I don't really know. I never thought about it before."

"I see," he said again, and did not realize until later how false the statement was. "I'm sorry to make you think about sad things, Stella, but will you tell me about that day . . . the day Mr. Baker died?"

She said, as she had said before, "There's nothing to tell."

"You went to Mass in the morning?"

"Yes, of course."

"And afterwards you had breakfast?"

"Yes. And then I helped Mum with the washing up and set the table for dinner." He couldn't help feeling that she offered the statement in a propitiatory way, as though she hoped he would accept it and not ask anything further. That was natural enough, wasn't it? But, of course, he had to go on.

"What did you do after that?"

"Nothing, really. I was in the dining room, so I stayed there, looking out of the window."

"Could you see Joe and Dick in the garden?"

"No, they were at the back of the house. The dining-room window looks out on the shrubbery at the side."

"Not a very interesting view."

She thought about that for a moment. "Mum says I'm always mooning around."

"Did you stay there until dinner time?"

"Not quite. Mum called me to help her dish up."

So far, so good. "Do you remember what was talked about when you were all at dinner?"

"No, I don't."

"When was your outing with Joe arranged?"

"I don't remember."

"Do you remember who suggested that you should go with him?"

"I think . . . perhaps . . . I did."

"That was at dinner time, wasn't it"

"Yes."

"So afterwards you went out together."

"Yes."

"Tell me about it."

"I don't know what you want me to say."

Careful now. "Just what happened while you were out. Who you saw, what you talked about."

"Yes . . . well . . . we had to walk to Cargate to catch the tram, and we met Bill Foster on the corner."

"Bill is a friend of Joe's, isn't he?"

"They know each other," said Stella cautiously.

"Did Joe stop to speak to him?"

"Yes; he said, 'Why don't you come with us?' or something like that. And Bill laughed and said, 'Not likely.' And then they walked away a few steps, and I couldn't hear what they were saying."

"Nothing at all?"

"Nothing at all. I'm sorry. And then Joe came back to me, and we crossed the road and caught the Lane's End tram. And we didn't meet anybody else we knew, all the afternoon."

She had been answering his direct questions readily enough, but that was obviously intended to end the matter. "But you had some conversation, didn't you, while you were walking?"

"Oh, yes, I expect we did," she said in an offhand way.

"What did you talk about?"

"I don't . . . I don't remember."

"Try to think, Stella. Was Joe his usual self? Did he seem quiet, worried about anything?"

"I didn't notice."

"You must have thought about it afterwards."

"Well, I did." The words came tumbling out now, so fast he could hardly catch them. "There wasn't anything . . . anything at all."

This time he was almost sure she was lying. He glanced at Sister Mary Dominic and caught what he interpreted as a warning glance. Even so, he thought he must press a little further. "It's important, Stella. It might help Joe if you could tell me—"

"I can't. I can't!"

"You didn't hear anything of his talk with Bill Foster?" he insisted. "And you don't remember what you talked about while you were on the moor?"

There was no answer except a sob. She was fumbling in the pocket of her dress, and when her hand came out empty he found his own spare handkerchief and handed it to her. She shook out the folds and buried her face in it. Sister Mary Dominic got up and came across the room to her side.

"I don't think she can help you, Mr. Maitland," she said. She put her hand on the girl's shoulder and shook it gently. "Crying won't help matters, Stella."

The two men were on their feet, too. "I'm sorry I upset her," said Antony in a troubled voice.

"I'm sure you are." There was a suggestion of irony that surprised him. "Can what she knows really help you, do you think?"

"There's no way of telling." He sounded disconsolate, and wasn't really surprised when Sister Mary Dominic gave him her encouraging smile. But there was a hint of reproach in her voice when she said,

"You are making her remember things that are better forgotten."

"Do you think that's the trouble?" he asked her, bluntly.

"The question is, whether she can forget." Stella's sobbing had quietened now, but she still held the handkerchief up to her eyes. "I only want to know, now, what happened after they got home again."

"Will you tell Mr. Maitland that, Stella?"

"And then I won't trouble you any more."

There was a long moment before she raised her head, and he saw her face streaked with tears. "Nothing happened," she said in a dead voice.

"You went in by the back door, didn't you?"

"Yes, and Winnie was there. In the kitchen. I was cold, so I stayed there, getting warm again. And Joe . . . went away."

"You didn't stop in the kitchen very long, though, did you?"

"Not very long."

"Where did you go then? To the playroom?"

"No, I went upstairs. Right upstairs, to my bedroom. And I didn't hear anything at all."

IX

"What did you mean?" asked Chris, when they were back in the hire car again and being driven towards the town. "Do you think she knows something?"

"That's what I was trying to find out." He did not sound impatient, only deadly weary.

"I don't see what it could be," said Conway, in a tone of discontent.

"Something she overheard, perhaps, between Joe and Bill Foster. Something, at a guess, that she thinks would make things worse for Joe."

"Could anything?" asked Chris bitterly. And was silent until they drew up outside the Midland Hotel. "You're dining with us tonight," he said then.

"I'm giving Star a great deal of bother." Chris only snorted at that, so he went on, "You said you have a flat in Ingleton Crescent, didn't you? I seem to have seen the name, not far from here."

"It's only about ten minutes walk if you take the towing path by the canal. But it's much farther by road; you'd better get a taxi."

"If you're thinking of the Walrus, he knocks off at midday on Saturdays."

"So you say."

"Anyway, he isn't a man of action. Not direct, physical action, I mean. If he tampered with your car—"

"So now you're beginning to doubt it."

"Not really. I was going to say, it looks as if he wants to stage an accident."

"You may be right," said Chris, unimpressed. "You'll find a taxi in the station yard."

"All right, I'll do that. What time?"

Chris glanced at his watch. "Would seven o'clock suit you?"

"Whenever you say." It would give him time for a bath and to phone Jenny. "I didn't mean to bully that child, you know."

"Don't worry. You were very kind to her," said Conway; and wondered why Antony grimaced suddenly, as at a disagreeable thought.

X

Afterwards he could not have said what prompted him to change his mind and walk round to the Conways. Perhaps it was sheer perversity, as Chris seemed inclined to believe; more likely it was because the day's activities had left him with a restless feeling that even his talk with Jenny had failed to dispel.

The sun had gone in, leaving the evening gray as well as chilly. He asked for directions at the desk; it sounded as if it would be easy enough to find the way. He had a good look round when he got outside, but the black Volkswagen was nowhere in sight, nor could he see anybody loitering suspiciously, with or without a moustache. He turned right along Swinegate and kept an eye open for "t' gin-nel," which he took to be a sort of narrow alleyway. Events having proved him right, he made his way between two warehouses, and found himself on the towpath with the canal gray and sullen beside him. And it was at this point, when his own footfalls were muffled on the packed earth, that he heard someone quite clearly coming down the alley behind him.

It didn't sound like Harry Fennister; too confident some-how, and anyway, too heavy for so small a man. Some in-nocent wayfarer, probably, who like himself had felt the need for exercise. All the same, it didn't do to take any chances. He moved quietly to stand close against the high, windowless wall of the warehouse, from which vantage point he would see, he hoped, before he was seen. And then the man who was following him came into view, and he saw that the precautions he had taken were not so much unnecessary as completely futile.

He'd been right in thinking the newcomer was a bigger man than Fennister . . . a giant would be a better descrip-tion. It wasn't just that he was tall—six foot six, at a guess —he was broad in proportion, or even, perhaps, out of proportion, and he looked in hard, fit condition, not an ounce of fat anywhere. As for the rest, he had thick, red-dish, curly hair, a rather flattened countenance, and hands like hams. (Which was probably, thought Antony, taking a deep breath, where the expression "ham fisted" came from, before it got distorted with use.) The big man turned then and saw him, and an expression of artless pleasure

112

irradiated his face, so that the name "Simple Simon" flashed across Maitland's mind, though he did not remember immediately where he had heard it. Prudence seemed to dictate that he didn't stay to find out, but something stronger than prudence kept him from headlong flight. "Human respect," Sister Mary Dominic might have called it, though he would have denied vehemently that he cared in the least whether the big man respected him or not.

"Now then!" said the newcomer in a pleased tone; he had a voice to match his size, deep and resonant. "You were waiting for me. Isn't that nice?"

This was a follow-up, of course, to Harry Fennister's practical joke; and that's where he'd heard the name "Simple Simon"; he was a friend of Harry's. And it seemed that they (whoever "they" were) were prepared to take whatever means came to hand, without bothering to simulate an accident, as he had believed they would prefer to do. He said, "Were you looking for me?" which afterwards he thought was a stupid question, and he began to edge away because it had occurred to him that if he was going into the canal anyway it might be better to do it of his own volition, rather than go in unconscious after Simon had finished with him. He wasn't in any doubt about the big man's intentions, and even without the complication of his shoulder and useless right arm he wouldn't have had much chance against a chap that size; as it was, the thing was hopeless from the start. But there was at least a chance (a good chance, even) that Simon couldn't swim. But first he must be sure . . .

"I've got a message for you," said Simple Simon, still apparently pleased with himself and his companion. He was coming forward as Antony went back, moving slowly and quietly so that he looked ridiculously like someone trying to make friends with a nervous animal.

"Have you, indeed?" said Maitland. He was getting near the bank of the canal now. "From your friend Harry Fennister . . . or someone else?"

For the first time the big man frowned. Perhaps the query, straightforward as it was, was too much for him. "Not from Harry," he said. And then, carefully, as if it was something he had memorized, "I haven't seen Harry today." And then he made a lunge forward, grasping for Maitland's lapel; and Maitland went back again rather more quickly than before. He avoided Simon's outstretched hand, but even as he did so he felt his foot slipping on the edge of the bank, and went down into the water rather sooner than he had intended, and much more inelegantly.

The water was cold and tasted muddy. He came up gasping and took a couple of strokes towards the opposite bank. Swimming one-armed was a clumsy business at best; clothed and wearing a raincoat it was hideously difficult, but at least there had been no echoing splash, so Simple Simon was evidently thinking twice at least before joining him.

He had paused, treading water, to look about him and weigh up the position, when he heard a shout and looked back to see another large man come pelting round the corner from the ginnel. His first thought was that this was too much of a good thing altogether, but to his surprise the second man, having apparently taken in the situation at a glance, came straight to the bank of the canal and called to him anxiously, "Mr. Maitland, are you all right?" Antony could not remember ever having seen him before.

"I'm not drowning, if that's what you mean," he replied, rather more tartly, perhaps, than the question warranted, but he was getting colder and more uncomfortable every minute. The man seemed reassured, and turned to Simple

Simon who was staring out across the water with his mouth open. "Now then!" said the newcomer unoriginally (a plainclothes detective, apparently, but how the devil did he come there?) "You're going to have to come along with me." The words seemed to have a galvanizing effect on Simon, who turned quickly and aimed a blow at the other man's head. Reluctantly, Antony began to swim back towards the bank from which he had entered the canal.

If the blow had landed, that would have ended matters then and there. The detective was a large man . . . nearly half as big as his assailant, thought Antony in gloomy exaggeration. As it was, he dodged neatly and answered by coming in close—a mistaken move, as it turned out—and aiming a shower of blows to the body that had no visible effect on Simon at all. He opened his arms and took the detective into a bearlike hug, probably as a preliminary to some further act of mayhem. Maitland paused a moment to collect a length of two-by-four timber that was floating near at hand, and heaved himself clumsily out of the water.

The thing seemed to be to act quickly, and the piece of wood was quite five feet long. Without pausing to see if some better idea might present itself he shoved it between Simon's legs, using it as a lever to trip him. The pair went down, still entwined, and the gray waters of the canal opened to receive them.

XI

He was late for dinner, of course, and overdressed for the occasion, having had to change back into his more formal, weekday clothes. Chris was inclined to say, "I told you so," when he heard what had happened; but

Star was as sympathetic an audience as anybody could wish to find. "The detective must have been very grateful to you," she said when he had finished.

"I daresay he may be, when he's had time to think things over," said Maitland, and grinned. "Luckily, he could swim. I gave him a hand up the bank, and then it took the two of us to get Simple Simon out. He was in a panic, which was just as well, because even with the handcuffs on him he wouldn't have been easy to deal with if he'd kept his head."

"What I don't understand," said Star reflectively, "is how did the detective come to be there?"

"That was your father's doing."

"Thank God for somebody with sense," said Chris piously.

"After our talk at lunchtime he put three men on to keeping an eye on Harry Fennister and his two cronies. Harry wasn't to be found, and they haven't heard from the one who was looking for Teddy Hill, either, but I was in luck that Simple Simon was easily located . . . it was his shadow that came to my rescue." He paused, and shared a smile between them. "Have you ever walked, dripping wet, through the lobby of an hotel. It seemed a mile from the door to the staircase."

"I expect it did," said Conway. He had his worried look, but he wasn't wasting any sympathy. "I've heard from the garage since I saw you, by the way."

"What had they to say?"

"Our friend the lorry driver was right. Someone had been tampering with the brakes."

"What exactly—?"

"The front nearside hydraulic hose had been partially cut through," said Chris, obviously quoting from memory, "and a piece of thin rubber tube placed over the cut and held by a couple of electricians cable clips. They think the rubber tube had been slit beforehand; anyway, it burst when I used the brakes rather suddenly, and that caused me to swerve across the road into the Jaguar's path."

"You might both have been killed," said Star, shuddering.

"Yes, but it's interesting that they didn't necessarily want to kill us," said Antony thoughtfully. "I mean, they couldn't rely on that . . . obviously, since we're still here."

"I expect they hoped for a bit more luck than they had, all the same. The thing is, what will they try next?"

"Nothing, if we're careful. How long would a job like that take?"

"About two minutes if it had been rehearsed and everything was to hand," Conway told him. "That's another thing, Inspector Duckett had some enquiries made at the Slubbers' Arms and found two relevant witnesses. One saw Harry come to the door of the bar and look round, presumably to see that we were well occupied . . . at least," he added, as Maitland was about to speak, "he saw a man with a walrus moustache and wearing greasy overalls, so I expect it was Harry, don't you?"

"He wasn't wearing them when we saw him earlier, but he could have had them in the car, I suppose. Who was the other witness?"

"Someone who actually saw him working on the Austin. But, of course, he thought it was a mechanic who had been called in to do some minor repair."

"It would need an expert, wouldn't it?"

"Harry used to hang around his local garage when he was younger, Inspector Duckett says . . . before he fell out of love with work."

"I see. Just like a jigsaw puzzle," said Maitland admiringly. "Everything dovetails nicely. I suppose with all your other preoccupations you didn't have time to speak to Mr. O'Donnell as well."

"I did, as a matter of fact."

"I might have known it. What had he to say?"

"A good deal, none of it to the point."

"Did he say when he saw Alfred Baker last?"

"On the Sunday morning, the day he died, after Mass."

"Not in the afternoon?"

"Positively no." Chris sighed. "Daresay he was telling the truth, you know."

"I daresay he was," agreed Antony sadly. After that, they talked of other things.

◬ Sunday, 22nd May

I

They didn't start work quite so early the following morning, ten thirty being the earliest hour at which Conway felt it would be reasonable to expect anyone to be available. Maitland lingered over his breakfast and read that the seamen's strike was still unresolved and that the United States had banned the export of highly sophisticated computers to France, which set his mind working on a wholly irrelevant tack. To his relief, the hotel had done wonders with his sodden clothing, which was delivered to his room dry and neatly pressed soon after ten o'clock.

They were going to see Peter Rawdon, who also lived in Cartwright Avenue, though a good deal farther from the main road than the Bakers did. "Though if you go along far enough," said Chris, as he came round the back of the car, "you come out into the Pateley Road." They had the same Austin Princess and the same driver as the day before.

"The farther off from England, the nearer is to France," Maitland said absently, apparently by way of agreement, though it was obvious that there was something else on his mind. It was sunny again that morning, and for the first time the sun seemed to have some warmth in it. "Is Rawdon going to hate us as much as O'Donnell did?" he added,

looking up at the house and making no immediate attempt to approach it.

"He didn't sound hostile when I phoned him," said Chris cautiously. The house was mock-Tudor, smaller than the rambling place where the Bakers lived and infinitely more tidy; a new-looking Mercedes was parked in front of the garage at the side of the house. "I suppose the thing to do is to find out."

Antony followed him up the short path to the front door. "You seem very full of resolution this morning," he complained. Chris took no notice of this but pressed the bell, and they heard a melodious chiming, deep inside the house. "Which do you think the maid will be, local or a foreigner?" But it was Rawdon himself who opened the door, and with very little delay.

"Come in, I was on the lookout for you," he said, when Chris had introduced himself and his companion. "We'll go into my study, and shan't be interrupted there." There was music coming from a room at the right, one of Brahms's symphonies, and Maitland caught a glimpse of chintz-covered chairs and the flicker of firelight as they passed. The room to which Rawdon led them was in its own way equally conventional, a man's room, with dark paneling and deep leather chairs. "Make yourselves comfortable," he invited hospitably, and himself took the chair at the right of the hearth. "I'm not very clear, I'm afraid, what I can do for you."

Maitland's first impression of him had been that he was a dapper little man. Certainly, he was dressed with a care that argued a fastidious taste, his fair hair had a sleekness that is not granted to every man, and his hands had a well-scrubbed, well-manicured look. But the smallness was an illusion; he was probably five foot ten or eleven, and though he had a compact frame, there was more than a hint of strength about it. An accountant, Chris had said, a partner in one of the best-known, most highly respected firms in Arkenshaw. Obviously, in his case, a profitable profession. It was difficult to see what he had in common with Alfred Baker, but that would doubtless emerge. In the meantime, as Chris had said, he didn't seem to be hostile, but he had a faintly supercilious look that might prove galling. "You knew Alfred Baker well," said Antony, at his most casual.

"I suppose you could say I was one of his closest friends."

"Then I'm sure you can tell us something about him."

"Yes, of course." He thought about it for a moment, his eyes fixed on Maitland's face. "You're acting for young Joe, aren't you? Then why—why on earth can what I tell you be of any use?"

"You don't object to being of use if you can?"

"I understand your position, I think, and I'd be the last person to condemn a man for trying to do his job." The air of condescension was very marked now. There is perhaps, thought Antony, ten years difference in our ages, but he is talking to me as if I were just out of kindergarten. He said, still mildly,

"Then you can have no objection to answering my questions."

"No objection at all."

"You played chess together, didn't you? I have been told that."

"Yes. Twice a week."

"Monday and Friday. Did you play here, or at his house?"

"Here, in this room." His tone added, "that should be obvious," but he only said, "The opportunities for concentration are greater." He paused for a moment before he went on. "You will forgive me, I know, but is this sort of detail really helpful?"

"I don't know. It may be," said Maitland vaguely. "One thing is apt to lead to another."

"Yes, I see. Now if you were to ask me about Joe—"

"What do you know about him?"

"Very little. He was causing Alfred some anxiety."

"In what way?"

"His friendship with Herbert Foster's son, Bill."

"Mr. Baker didn't approve?"

"For one thing, there was the difference in their positions. Bill is still at school, but he has more pocket money than is good for him, while Joe had his way to make."

"You said, 'for one thing'—"

"Yes, well, for another there's Bill's reputation."

"Somebody told me he is seventeen."

"If you're thinking that's too young, I can only say he's precocious. He'd have been in trouble once or twice if Herbert hadn't smoothed things over."

"What sort of trouble?"

"Once it was creating a disturbance. A bunch of youngsters, drunk or drugged, I wouldn't know. Another time there was a raid on the Peppermint Stick, but in the end no charges were laid."

"More shadow than substance."

"You may be right."

"Was Joe involved in any way?"

"Not directly, no. Only as one of Bill's Foster's known associates. But I know it worried Alfred."

"You think that's why Joe killed him?"

"How can I say? It was certainly a cause of friction between them."

"I see. What do you think of Joe?"

"That's an impossible question now." He dismissed it

impatiently, but after a moment he relented sufficiently to add, "I used to think he was a nice boy, rather dull."

"Has he a temper?"

"I have never seen any sign of it. But I remember Alfred told me he had been in trouble for fighting once or twice, while he was still at school."

"Can we get back to Mr. Baker, then? As such a close friend—"

"I knew him better than I know any other member of his family, certainly."

"You had at least one interest in common."

"More than that. Alfred was a very unusual man, Mr. Maitland. In other circumstances . . . well, perhaps I mean, if he had had more opportunities open to him when he was young, he might have gone a very long way. He had a good brain."

"Wasted in his job, you think?"

"I wouldn't say that. I'm sure Foster found him invaluable."

"You haven't mentioned the most remarkable thing about him."

"The children. He'd have liked a family of his own, I expect."

"But you think, as a group, they were happy? He wasn't too demanding, for instance?"

"If I could still trust my own judgment, I should say they were nice kids, well brought up." But his tone denied the implied self-criticism.

"That doesn't quite answer—"

"Not too demanding. I can't answer for what one or another of them may have felt, of course."

"Another thing I'm interested in is Mr. Baker's financial position."

"I don't see the relevance of that, I'm afraid." He waited,

but when Maitland said nothing, went on in a dissatisfied tone. "In any event, I know nothing about it, except that he was always hard up, as you might expect."

"Did he ever talk to you about his work?"

"Only in the most general terms. I imagine it was confidential, don't you? Apart from our chess games—which can engender more conversation than you might, perhaps, suppose—we talked of books and world affairs. He was a well-read man."

"When did you last see him, before his death?"

"We had our usual game on the Friday evening."

"Did he seem to have anything on his mind?"

"Nothing in particular. He was never a lively man."

"And that was the last time? I am trying to find if somebody saw him the afternoon he died."

"I thought . . . I understood . . . certainly *I* did not see him, Mr. Maitland." All the time they talked there was very little change of expression on Rawdon's face; Antony wondered whether this in itself might not be regarded as a sign of contempt.

"You made the funeral arrangements, I believe."

"I did what I could for Agnes. Somebody had to see to things."

"There was also the question of winding up his estate."

"Foster saw to that, as was natural. I don't imagine he had much to leave."

"He might have been insured."

"What makes you think—?"

"Something Mr. Foster told us. He said Alfred Baker was an expert in insurance matters, didn't he, Chris?"

"Something like that," Conway agreed. He sounded as if he was doing so to be obliging, without very much recollection of the conversation that was referred to.

"So it seems strange, if he was an expert, that he neglected his own affairs."

"That is nothing to do with me . . . or with you, Mr. Maitland."

"But it might be interesting," Maitland persisted, apparently oblivious of the snub. He saw from the corner of his eye that Chris was frowning.

"I cannot see that it would help you at all," said Rawdon positively.

"You may be right. Have you—had you any common friends?"

"Not that I am aware."

"Did he mention—?"

"We were not in the habit of discussing personalities."

"Except Joe."

"Well . . . I imagine the matter was very much on his mind."

There was more than a hint in his tone of patience exhausted. Antony smiled apologetically and pulled himself out of his chair. "We won't keep you any longer, Mr. Rawdon. I'm grateful for your help."

The words acted like magic. The slight stiffness in Peter Rawdon's manner vanished, and though he came to his feet with alacrity, it was with apologies that almost sounded genuine that he had been so little use. They parted on a note of cordiality, but Antony was thoughtful as they went back to the waiting car.

Chris stopped to give the driver directions. "I can't see," he said, as he joined Maitland on the back seat, "why you should have mentioned the possibility of Baker being insured."

"Can't you?"

"If he had been, Foster would have told us."

"That's what I thought," Maitland agreed readily enough. But he did not seem inclined for any further discussion. He looked over his shoulder from time to time as they went, but there was nothing to indicate that they were being followed.

II

This time Herbert Foster must have been waiting for them in the hall, he opened the front door so promptly after they rang. "I should just like a word with you, Maitland, if you don't mind," he said, and led the way into a pretty, conventional sitting room, which probably reflected his wife's taste rather than his own.

"It's really Bill we wanted to see," Conway told him, when an awkward little silence had lengthened itself unduly.

"Yes, so you explained to me," said Foster in a hurried way. "But I was puzzled . . . I was wondering—"

"As Joe's close friend, and his contemporary, he may be able to help us more than anyone else."

"But there is not—I should like to be assured that there is not—any question of calling him as a witness."

"None that I can foresee," said Chris, and he glanced at Maitland for confirmation. Antony nodded and said, equally cautiously,

"For my own information . . . so far as I know."

Foster said, "Yes, I understand," but he did not sound as if the answers contented him. He looked from one of them to the other, and his uneasiness was so obvious as to be almost a tangible thing.

"Was Alfred Baker insured?" asked Maitland, changing the subject with an abruptness that startled both his companions.

"No. That is, there was a small policy . . . enough to cover the funeral expenses."

"Nothing more?"

"No." He seemed happier now. "I think he would have told you that he couldn't afford the premiums."

"I see. When did you see him for the last time?"

"At the office on Friday afternoon."

"Not during the weekend?"

"No." The happiness had been short-lived. "I can't quite see—"

"I was wondering if you had observed anything unusual in his manner."

"Nothing at all. No."

"Then if we could just have a word with Bill, Mr. Foster—"

"Of course, of course. I—er—I persuaded him to stay at home until you came."

"He doesn't want to see us?"

"Nothing like that. I didn't mean to imply—" He broke off; perhaps he was contemplating the truth, or otherwise, of this statement. "It is just that he is puzzled, as I am—" The sentence trailed off into silence as he made for the door. "If you will sit down, both of you, I will send him to you."

But it was quite five minutes before Bill Foster appeared. Maitland wasn't quite sure what he had been expecting . . . something pretty odd. What he saw was a young man very like his father: the same large frame, the same rather small head. The straight, dark hair was overlong, certainly, but not outrageously so. His clothes were different too, but there was nothing out of the way in the heavy green pullover he was wearing, or the gray flannels, which were clean and well pressed. But there *was* something wrong, something Antony couldn't define immediately. He was fidgety, didn't know what to do with his hands, but that wasn't the whole story.

They sat around the hearth. The fire was laid, but not

lighted; that morning the central heating seemed to be enough. Bill had said nothing after a rather grudging good-morning, and this time Conway did not attempt to break the silence. After a while Maitland said,

"You're a friend of Joe Hartley."

"He was a good guy."

"Why the past tense? He isn't dead, you know."

"Might as well be." His response came readily enough, but with an economy of words that wasn't exactly encouraging.

"As far as you're concerned, you mean?"

"Well . . . he's in prison."

"But the length of time he spends there may depend on —may depend on what you have to tell me, for instance." He wasn't surprised at the boy's terse replies, he'd been expecting that. But the odd thing, the thing he had noticed without being able to put a name to it, was the extraordinary shiftiness of Bill's eyes. It wasn't that they wouldn't meet his directly, that wasn't too unusual, but that they seemed never to be still for an instant.

"I know what you're after. You're looking for an out for Joe."

"That's one way of putting it. As you're a friend of his—"

"I was."

"Not any longer?"

"You can't be friends with a guy you never see."

"Still, you wish him no harm?"

"No." He laughed suddenly, and for a second his eyes met Maitland's before they shifted away.

"What's the joke?"

"I doubt if you'd understand."

"Try me."

"All this time the Bakers have been on at Joe for not being more particular in his choice of friends."

"*And lo! Ben Adhem's name led all the rest.*" Bill

128

frowned at him. "And now you're the one who has been getting into bad company," Maitland explained, and the boy gave a quick nod of comprehension.

"That's what I meant."

"How long have you known Joe?"

"All my life, nearly. I didn't see so much of him until he left school."

"You're still at the grammar school, aren't you?"

"Yes. Taking my 'A' levels this year."

"Going to pass?" The laconic style was beginning to affect Maitland's speech too.

"Shouldn't think so."

"What had you and Joe in common?"

Again there was the brief flash of amusement. "Buggered if I know."

"Tell me about his other friends."

"Don't know them. I've seen him about with a couple of firebugs."

"Fire—?" The rather bad pun took a moment to penetrate. "Pupils of St. Blaise's?"

"Old Boys. I think."

"What do you suppose they did when they were together?"

"Went for a walk. Took in a flick. I don't know."

"You do not yourself care for walking."

"I've better things to do with my time."

"Did Joe belong to any clubs?"

"Not unless you count the Peppermint Stick. Some of us hang out there."

"Joe among you?"

"He's been there."

"Did he ever bring his sister with him?"

"Win? Not on your life."

"Some other girl, or girls?"

"Not lately."

"You mean, his habits had changed?"

Bill took time to think that out. He seemed faintly puzzled. His fingers drummed on the arm of his chair.

"I suppose you could say so."

"Since when?"

"I don't know exactly. About a year. More than that perhaps."

"Can you think of anything to account for the change?"

"Come to think of it, perhaps they'd been on at him to spend more time with the kids."

"They? The Bakers?"

"That's right. He'd a proper sense of duty."

"Would you say he had a belligerent nature?"

"Joe? Easygoing as they come."

"He got into two fights, at least, at school."

"I'm not saying he couldn't be roused. Just, it wasn't easy."

"Do you remember what the trouble was about?"

"Someone taking the mickey out of him about the family, I expect."

"Baker's dozen?"

"Well, you must admit, they carried it rather far."

"Why do you suppose he killed his foster father?"

"How should I know?"

"Because you probably know him better than anybody else."

"I wouldn't say that."

"What would you say then?"

Bill hesitated. Perhaps he felt it was time for a change of course. "Young Stella was with him that day."

"You met them, didn't you? I've been meaning to ask you about that."

"There's nothing to tell."

"Come now, you must see it's important."

"Why?"

"There was no quarrel between Joe and Mr. Baker at dinner time. Joe went out with Stella immediately after dinner, and ten minutes after they got home again Mr. Baker was dead. Stella says you're the only person they met—"

"You're saying Joe had a grievance against the old man. It might have been the other way about."

"I hadn't forgotten that. Do you know of any possible reason—?"

"No, I don't."

"Then we must content ourselves with what you do know. If Joe had some—some confession to make to his foster father—"

"I don't know of anything like that."

"What did you talk about that afternoon?"

"Nothing in particular."

"You must remember something of the conversation."

"Well, he asked me if I was going with them, but that was only a joke. He knew I wouldn't."

"Did you make any counter proposal?"

"There was a good movie on at the Gaumont. He could easily have sent the kid home."

"But he wouldn't?"

"No. Said he'd promised. So I said I'd be at the Peppermint Stick that evening, and he said, 'See you,' and off he went." There was an air of improvisation about this that Maitland didn't quite like; also Bill Foster's eyes were fixed on his for the first time for several seconds together, and he didn't like that either. He wanted the truth, and he hadn't the faintest idea if he was getting it or not.

"What did Joe think about drugs?" he asked, and was pleased to see that for the first time the boy was obviously disconcerted by the abrupt question.

"What do you mean?"

"Just what I say."

"Well, he had this thing about keeping fit, you know."

"You're saying that he disapproved of them for his own use."

"I don't know that he approved of them at all. The question never arose."

"Did it not?" Perhaps it was the dryness of Maitland's voice that made Bill glance at him quickly and then away again. One hand went up to tug at the roll collar of his pullover, as though it had suddenly become too tight for him. "I'm not concerned to moralize," Maitland went on, "but I should like to know where you get your supplies."

"I never said—"

"Are you telling me you don't use marijuana?"

"There's no harm—"

"You didn't listen to what I said, you know."

"Grass is easy enough to come by."

"And . . . heroin, for instance?"

"I don't—"

"You really should listen to the question," Maitland complained.

"I could get it easily enough if I wanted," said Bill with an air of bravado.

"And pass it on as easily," said Antony casually.

"I didn't say—"

"Don't tell me you've never given a friend a fix if he wanted it."

"Oh . . . well! Not heroin though."

"For a price?"

"No!" That was the first time he had been startled into vehemence. "They'd pay me back when they could."

"You still haven't told me where your supplies come from."

"Why should I?"

"That isn't an easy question to answer."

"It can't concern Joe."

"Can't it?" Maitland's tone was quiet, but there was no doubt that he had succeeded in riveting Bill Foster's attention.

"I told you Joe didn't use the stuff."

"But he was tolerant of your addiction."

"I can take it or leave it alone."

"I must take your word for that. And also for the fact that you have never engaged in peddling drugs. But can you say the same for Joe?"

"He certainly never . . . oh, no, that's too stupid even to think about. Joe, of all people!"

"Can you be sure of that? Has it never struck you that he was rather unusually flush with money, say?"

"He was always careful. But it isn't that . . . no, really it isn't. He was too . . . well, not the sort of person . . . too square."

"I see." It sounded like the truth. He thought, perhaps, it was the truth. Was it worth antagonizing the boy by giving him a warning? He came to his feet as he said, "Does your father know that you use marijuana . . . sometimes?"

"He never asked me." Bill's air of bravado was very marked now. "I suppose he doesn't. Are you going to tell him?"

"No. If you haven't the sense yourself—"

"You said you weren't going to moralize."

"So I did. I'm sorry." He went to the door and turned there and smiled. "You may even find a tendency in that direction in yourself as you get older."

"Don't count on it."

"I won't. Good-bye, and thank you for your help." He pulled the door open and went out into the hall.

III

Chris Conway had had no time to do any spadework on the next three interviews ... the St. Blaise's boys who had been mentioned in their talk with Monsignor Carter. They saw Keating before lunch—the family lived over the shop in Cargate—and his parents were curious, but on the whole cooperative. But for all the help he could give, they might as well have vetoed the talk altogether. Wilfred—a slight, rather nervous boy with spots—could remember the fight all right, but not the cause of it. Or so he maintained. Maitland and Conway went to the Swan and Signet for beer and sandwiches, and neither of them was in a very cheerful frame of mind.

Illingworth and Carter lived in the same row of terrace houses, just round the corner from the Bakers' home. When he thought back to the matter afterwards Antony could never remember very clearly which of them was which. One of them had rabbit teeth and a father who insisted on sitting in on the interview; the other was sturdy and good-humored, and his parents were good-humored, too, and seemed to take it for granted that the two visitors had come with no very sinister purpose in mind. Antony knew, because he found the envelope on which he had scribbled a few notes in his pocket that night, that Illingworth remembered the second fight ("Keating was kidding him about that picture in the Universe"); while Carter hadn't even been in school that day, had only heard afterwards what had happened, but remembered the earlier occasion quite well. "Not that I can tell you what it was all about," he said, "though I expect I knew at the time. Something Joe happened to feel strongly about, I expect."

"That means he's inclined to hold strong opinions."

"Oh, yes, quite a chap for lost causes."

But neither of them could think of any reason why Joe

134

should have killed his foster father; there might have been something in his conduct that Mr. Baker disapproved of, but it certainly wouldn't be anything illegal . . . Joe just wasn't the type. (How many times have I heard *that* said about one of my less innocent clients?) And they both in turn admitted that they hadn't seen so much of him lately, but while Illingworth (upon reflection, wasn't he the one with the rabbit teeth?) thought he must have found himself a girl friend, Carter had given very little consideration to the matter . . . it was just one of those things.

"We're not getting anywhere," said Chris as they walked back to the car again after the second interview. "I've fixed it so that we can see Joe next, but do you still want to?"

"More than ever." He gave a sidelong glance at his companion. "The basic problem hasn't changed, you know. And it was your idea to bring me here to deal with it."

"So you keep reminding me."

"Well, then!"

"If Joe has been mixed up with a drug ring, that won't exactly endear him to the jury," said Conway, sounding stubborn.

"I could put forward an argument," Maitland told him. They had reached the car now, and he came to a halt by the nearside door. "In any case, I see no reason to suppose anything of the sort."

"But, damn it all," said Chris, for once moved out of his customary composure, "there must be some reason for what happened to the car and for Simple Simon's attack on you last night."

"Well, but I don't think it's that." He glanced up and down the road as he spoke. "Do you realize, nobody's following us today?"

"I thought perhaps they'd got discouraged."

"Or somebody doesn't like paying time and a half."

"Perhaps that's it." Conway's mind was obviously still on Joe Hartley. "If you don't agree with me about the drugs, what *do* you think about his motive?"

"I haven't any idea at all."

"Then why—?"

"He may be more amenable after a day in court." Maitland stopped to open the car door. He didn't sound particularly optimistic, and as things turned out that was just as well.

IV

It was obvious that Joe was on the defensive as soon as he came into the interview room. "I told you it was no good," he said. "I told you that to start with, Mr. Conway."

"We're doing our best for you, Joe."

"Yes, I know." He slumped down into the chair at the end of the table. "If you'd done what I wanted—"

Maitland looked up from the torn envelope on which he was scribbling. "What was that?" he asked in his mildest voice.

"To let me plead 'guilty' and be done with it."

"You would have preferred to dispense with the formality of a trial?"

"Yes, I would. If things were different . . . but they aren't. You know I killed him."

"No one has tried to suggest anything else."

"No, but . . . you're trying to make out I wasn't responsible, somehow."

"Were you?" Maitland's tone sharpened. "Tell me honestly, Joe, were you quite yourself . . . was it a calm, deliberate act, when you killed him?"

"Of course I wasn't calm." He broke off, and gave his counsel a lowering look. "You're not catching me like that."

"I suppose not. Tell me, did you enjoy yourself in court?"

He knew as he asked the question that it was an unfair

136

one. Joe evidently agreed with him, and his answer came with ill-suppressed violence. "You know it was hell."

"Yes, I was afraid of that. If you'd change your mind it might make a difference—"

"Change my mind . . . what about?"

"About confiding in us."

He had got no further than that when Joe interrupted him furiously. "I killed him, that's all that matters. Why should you care *why*?"

"I can only repeat what Mr. Conway said just now. We're trying to help."

"Well, it wouldn't help . . . even if I told you."

"Won't you let me be the judge of that?"

"No!" His hands were clenched on the table in front of him; now he relaxed deliberately, leaned back in his chair, and looked at once older and more vulnerable. "I don't mean to seem ungrateful—"

"Forget it," Maitland snapped. He got up and began to pace about the room, which was not large enough to give his restlessness much scope. "It's a matter of professional pride," he said, improvising. "We don't like being made fools of. Do we?" he appealed to Chris.

"No more than the next man," said Conway, trying to keep the mystification out of his voice.

Joe's eyes were following Maitland's movement: three paces to the dusty window, five paces across the width of the room again. "I don't know what you're talking about," he said.

"*You're* not enjoying yourself in court. What about us?"

"I've told you I'm grateful."

"To hell with your gratitude. I'm told you're a fighter, Joe. Give me half a chance—"

"I killed him."

"I'm not disputing the fact. I want to know why."

"Well, I won't tell you. Even if it would help . . . I can't."

137

His voice went up on the assertion. Maitland came back to stand behind his chair.

"We've been talking to your friend, Bill Foster," he said quietly.

"Have you?" The controls were back on again now, clamped down hard.

"You met him that day, when you were out with Stella."

"So I did."

"What did you talk about?"

"Didn't he tell you?" Maitland said nothing, just stood looking at him. "I think he said something about seeing me that evening. I don't really remember."

"At the Peppermint Stick?"

"Yes."

"Mr. Baker didn't like that association, did he?"

"Not much."

"Why not?"

"Mr. Foster was his employer. He wouldn't think it suitable."

"Besides, there was always the chance you might get hooked on drugs as well."

"Dad didn't know—"

"Didn't he?" asked Maitland, when Joe dried up. From the corner of his eye he saw Chris Conway make an abrupt movement and turned to look at him. "Is there something you want to ask?"

"I think . . . yes, there is," said Chris firmly. "Some queer things have been happening since Mr. Maitland started asking questions, Joe."

"What sort of things?"

"Someone tampered with my car, to cause an accident. It was sheer luck neither of us was hurt."

Joe was frowning, but he didn't say anything immediately. "I'm sorry, of course, but I don't see what it's got to do with me."

"Wait a bit. Later in the day Mr. Maitland was attacked."

"What happened?"

"I ended up in the canal," said Antony lightly. His eyes were on Joe's face. Joe was watching Chris Conway.

"I still don't see—"

"It made us wonder what somebody had to hide." Chris was intent on his argument. "Something that might come to light when we started asking questions about you, Joe."

"There's nothing—"

"Are you sure of that? If you've been mixed up in something shady, it might not be altogether to your disadvantage to tell us about it, you know."

"What *sort* of thing?" asked Joe again.

"Drugs, for instance."

"But I don't—"

"There's a problem in the town. Someone's distributing them. And if you were mixed up in it and Mr. Baker found out—"

He let the sentence trail into silence. Joe glanced quickly at Maitland and then back at Conway again. "Suppose I said that was it?"

"It might be the best thing you could do," said Chris seriously. (So he took my point, Maitland thought, even though I didn't elaborate it.) "A first offense, your age would count in your favor. And though it wouldn't excuse what you did, it might go a certain way towards explaining why you lost your head."

"Yes, I see," said Joe. "Well—" Maitland pulled out his chair, scraping it against the worn linoleum, and sat down again.

"We shall want particulars of your associates, Joe," he said.

"I'm not a sneak."

"You're not a schoolboy either. If we're to persuade the court to take a lenient view—"

"I don't think you could, anyway."

"As Mr. Conway says, we could try. He's made out a good case, but we need your help, too."

"I don't know anything really."

"Come now. There are some things you can tell us. How long have you been involved?"

"About . . . since soon after I left school."

"How was the first approach made to you?"

"At the . . . I don't remember."

"Think about it. At the Peppermint Stick? At a football match? At a church social?"

"Outside the Peppermint Stick. A man was waiting when I left one night; he walked down the street with me."

"Who was it?"

"I don't know his name."

"What was he like?"

"Oh . . . small and dark . . . a rather sharp sort of face."

"And—?"

"He asked me if I was interested in making some money, and I said I was. So he told me how I could."

"Just like that!" said Maitland admiringly. "What did you do with it? Don't tell me you saved it," he added, "because we know you didn't."

"I spent it."

"What on?"

"This and that."

"Very informative. Tell us about some of the gang whose names you *did* know."

"I never . . . it was all nicknames. Mugger, and Flash, and Duke."

"How was the distribution arranged?"

140

"There's a hollow tree in the park . . . I could show you. I used to find a package there and a list of names."

"And who did you pass the stuff on to?"

"Some of the kids."

"You knew *their* names."

"Of course I did. But I don't want to tell you."

"Bill Foster?"

"No, not Bill."

Maitland looked at Chris and smiled at him. "Well?" he asked.

"You've convinced me." Conway sat back and looked at his client thoughtfully. "I don't admire your taste in fiction, Joe."

"I wasn't . . . don't you believe me?"

"Not a word."

"There's probably a hollow tree in the park," said Maitland, with the air of one who is trying to be fair.

"Yes, I daresay. I admit it was my idea, Joe, I can't blame you for taking it up, but you aren't a good enough liar."

"If you'd just let me alone," said Joe, sulky again. "That's all I want. Just let me alone."

"Tell me one thing then, before we go," Maitland suggested. "You were in trouble at school a few times for fighting."

"Once or twice."

"And in each case, I've been told, you were the aggressor."

"Was I? I don't remember."

"Take my word for it then."

"How would *that* help you?"

"You're a peaceable sort of chap, aren't you? I'd like to know what you think is worth fighting about." His tone was casual; there seemed nothing about the remark to make Joe change color, but he flushed a dusky red. He said, even more doggedly than before,

"I don't remember. I don't suppose it was worth remembering."

And with that, it seemed, they would have to be content.

V

There was still no sign that they were being followed. "That didn't get us very far, did it?" said Chris as they drove back towards the hotel. "So there we are, without any more leads to follow that I can see." He added insistently when Maitland did not immediately reply, "That's right, isn't it? The drugs were a red herring after all."

"Unless you think Joe is clever enough to do a double bluff."

"I don't think that. And nor do you," he added accusingly. "We've gone as far as we can."

Antony seemed to shake himself out of his abstraction. "I've just one more question to ask before we quite despair," he said. "If I went to Old Peel Farm this evening, should I find Grandma at home?"

"Grandma?" said Chris. It was more like a yelp than anything else.

"Why not?"

"Well . . . no reason at all, I suppose. It's just that she doesn't know anything about the case, so I can't see how she can help you."

"She knows everything that goes on in Arkenshaw," said Maitland as though he hadn't listened to the objection. "Far more than the inspector does." He paused and added with a smile, when Conway showed no signs of comprehension, "I'm not going to ask her to read my horoscope, or Joe's."

"I didn't imagine . . . of course you can see her if you want to. But we're dining with Dad, all of us."

"I hadn't forgotten, I'm looking forward to seeing him again. But afterwards—"

"Oh, very well," said Chris, not quite graciously. Antony gave him a sidelong glance, and asked solemnly, "Do you think I dare quote Chesterton to her?"

"To Grandma? I shouldn't think it would be advisable. What is it this time?" said Chris in a resigned tone.

"Feast on wine or fast on water, and your honour shall stand sure. She *will* give me sergeant-major's tea," Antony complained.

"If you really think her parsnip wine would be preferable . . . I've warned you once about that."

"According to Chesterton . . . it goes on, you know:

> *If an angel out of heaven*
> *Gives you other things to drink,*
> *Thank him for his kind attentions,*
> *Go and pour them down the sink."*

"I don't imagine Grandma holds with angels." Chris was grinning now. "So perhaps you'd better keep your quotations to yourself." He glanced at his watch as the car drew up outside the Midland Hotel. "We'll call for you at ten to seven. Will that be all right?"

It was five past five when Maitland walked into the lobby of the hotel. The depression caused by the visit to the prison still clung to him, and he was more tired than he would have cared to admit . . . perhaps it was with the awareness of failure. At home, Jenny and Uncle Nick would be having tea by the fire, unless the spring afternoon was warm enough to dispense with one. For all the good he had done he might as well have been there with them . . .

He thought as he went in that the lobby was deserted, except for a somnolent clerk behind the desk; which was only to be expected at that hour on a Sunday afternoon. It wasn't until he had got half-way towards the staircase that he heard his name spoken, and felt a small hand clutch at his arm. He turned sharply and saw Stella looking up at him with beseeching eyes.

She was, perhaps, the last person he had expected to see. He said, "Why . . . hallo," seeking some way of reassuring her, even in the midst of his own surprise. "Where did you spring from?"

"I was waiting for you."

He had to bend his head to catch the words at all. "Are you alone?"

"Yes. Oh, yes." But she glanced round as though she expected to see someone she knew, lurking in a corner.

"Does your mother—does Mrs. Baker know you're here?" She shook her head; her lips were set in a thin, stubborn line. For a moment he saw her, or thought he saw her, as she would be in maturity. "Or Winnie?" he asked insistently.

"I didn't tell anyone. I just want to talk to you."

He remembered how she had cried when he had pressed his questions at the convent the day before. Now he wasn't at all sure that he wanted to hear the replies. "That's very nice of you, Stella. I expect you'd like some tea. We can—"

"Please . . . I don't want anything." She was a child again, and her problem—surely—could only be a childish one. But even as he thought that, he knew it was a dangerous line of argument.

"Let's go into the lounge anyway."

"No . . . I want . . . there might be people there."

She was still clutching his sleeve, and he put up his hand to cover hers. "There's never anybody in the smaller

144

lounge," he said. "We could have that to ourselves." He was trying to speak in a calm, matter-of-fact way, and finding it difficult. Stella's whole body was quivering, and something of her nervousness seemed to be communicating itself to him.

"It isn't worthwhile. I'll just tell you, and then I'll go." A man and a woman came in through the swing doors, and the woman glanced at them curiously as they went across to the stairs. But Stella was probably right, they could be as private here as anywhere, and afterwards he could tackle the problem of getting her home.

"Take your time," he said. "There's no hurry."

"No," she agreed. Somehow she sounded desolate, as though she had retreated to a great distance away from him. But then she broke the lengthening silence with a sudden burst of confidence. "I don't want . . . anything dreadful . . . to happen to Joe."

"Neither do I, Stella. Do you know something that could help him?"

"I don't know. You said . . . you seemed to think . . . if you knew what happened that afternoon—"

"I want to know, very badly." That was as near as he could get to it, he wasn't even sure if it was the truth. The knowledge might help him, and it might hinder him. Was it even fair to Joe to let her go on? She had released her grip on his sleeve, but her hand still lay passive in his own. She said, looking away from him now, past his shoulder,

"I didn't tell you the truth yesterday." She caught herself up on the statement. "I didn't tell you *all* the truth."

"That isn't so very dreadful." Her eyes met his again, and he thought they looked reproachful. "I mean, it's easily remedied, isn't it, now you're here?"

"It isn't easy," she said, contradicting him sadly. Her lip quivered, and he saw the tears welling up into her eyes.

145

"It's what we talked about . . . what I told Joe that afternoon."

"I see," said Maitland gently.

"I don't suppose you do." She closed her eyes tightly, so that the tears trembled on her eyelashes for a moment and then began to run slowly down her cheeks. His hand tightened on hers, but whatever the trouble might be she was bearing it alone, in some cold world of her own imagining, and he had a feeling that nothing he said or did would be of any comfort to her.

"Tell me anyway," he invited, and she said, still with her eyes shut against a world she seemed to find unfriendly.

"I told him I'm going to have a baby."

And as she spoke the tiled floor seemed to shudder under their feet; there was a sort of rumbling roar that filled the air all around them; and the crystal chandelier that hung in the center of the lobby jangled wildly for a moment and then came crashing down barely a yard from where they were standing.

VI

For a moment after that everything was very still and very silent. Without the artificial light the hall was dim, though it would still be daylight outside. Antony found himself on the floor with Stella underneath him; his reactions hadn't slowed that much, it seemed, after twenty years of peace. He got up now, moving rather slowly and stiffly, because he had jolted his shoulder and it was giving him hell. He reached out his left hand to Stella, and pulled her to her feet. She looked dazed, which wasn't surprising, and the tears were still wet on her cheeks.

The clerk at the reception desk was staring at the damage with his mouth open. As the dust settled Maitland could see that a small group of people had come out of

146

the lounge at the right of the hall, and another, larger group through the service door. Everybody was talking at once. "Very near . . . seemed as if it was right over our heads . . . takes you back, doesn't it?" A man pushed his way in with such force as to leave the door rotating behind him. "Call an ambulance, will you, lad," he shouted to the clerk. "There's three people hurt in the streets."

To his eternal credit, the clerk grabbed the telephone without wasting time on questions. The crowd that had gathered—perhaps twenty people in all, but it seemed like a crowd, the way they were milling about—were not so forbearing. They clustered around the newcomer, demanding loudly, "What's the matter? . . . What happened? . . . Where . . .?"

"There's been an explosion, that's what," said the man from the street scornfully. (As if they shouldn't have known that for themselves.) "That's what hurt them, see . . . flying masonry. Half the wall's down."

All this time Antony had been holding Stella in the shelter of his arm. She hadn't said a word. "If I leave you for a minute will you stay here? Will you be all right? I just want to see what's happened." She nodded without speaking; he didn't trust her calmness, but even if he stayed with her he couldn't put his questions now. Not until things had settled down a bit and they knew what had happened. He turned to speak to a woman standing near. "Will you keep an eye on her for me? I won't be long." He was beginning to be afraid . . .

At the foot of the stairs he encountered the hotel manager; they went up side by side. "To the left, I think," said Maitland as they reached the landing, and the manager said, "So do I," breathlessly, and before they had taken two steps in that direction they knew they were right. One of the heavy wooden doors, a little twisted out of shape, lay half across the corridor, leaning drunkenly

147

against the wall. There was dust everywhere, almost enough to blind them, and a peculiar, acrid smell. The corridor lights were burning, they must be on a different circuit from the chandelier downstairs, but they hardly helped at all; it was as if they were shining through a thick blanket of yellow fog.

As they got a bit nearer, "I'm not sure, but I think it's my room," Maitland said, and the manager—whose name he never discovered, then or later—made an oddly deprecatory tutting sound that might almost have been an apology. That was when Antony first saw that someone was lying half under the heavy door. One of the chambermaids, from her black and white uniform. At the same moment a billow of smoke from the empty room set them coughing, and they heard the crackle of flames.

The bed was on fire. The manager, with another of his wordless exclamations, seized the nearest fire extinguisher and brought it into play with as much aplomb as if he had been rehearsing the act every day for years. Maitland was left to see what he could do for the injured woman, but he couldn't lift the door alone. It seemed an age before the other man rejoined him, rubbing his hands in a satisfied way.

Between them they managed to extricate her. If the corridor had been wider she would have been crushed under the weight of the wood; as it was, it might turn out to be no worse than a case of bad concussion. "She must have been right outside the door when it happened," said the manager, stating the obvious. And then, more practically, "I'll go down and tell them we need the ambulance men up here too."

Left alone, Maitland stood for a moment, looking down at the unconscious woman; but there was nothing he could do to help her, nothing that mightn't make matters worse. He couldn't very well leave her, either, though it was time he looked for Stella again. He trod delicately to the gaping doorway, conscious that with every step he was disturbing the thick layer of dust that carpeted the corridor. The man downstairs had exaggerated only a little when he said, "half the wall's down." The outer wall of the room had disappeared completely, except for a jagged frieze of brick, and as he watched another brick detached itself and crashed down to the pavement below. Somebody shouted . . . anxiously? . . . in protest? . . . and then there was nothing to be heard but the voices of the onlookers again, drifting up from the street, a murmuring no louder than the sound of waves breaking on the shore.

It was certainly his room. The bathroom door was open, which was probably why it had escaped the full effect of the blast; however that might be, his dressing gown was hanging there, apparently unharmed. Everything else was a shambles, as though some giant, destructive hand had seized and twisted wood and metal into some odd, impressionistic design. The bed was charred, and gray runnels of water were dripping from it and cutting their channels through the dust. He backed away, coughing, and retreated a few paces down the corridor where the air was clearer.

They were lucky—damned lucky—that the whole thing hadn't gone up in flames.

It was ten minutes later when the ambulance men arrived, with the manager in anxious attendance, and relieved him of his vigil. It was queer to see the lobby looking almost as usual, if you excepted the remains of the chandelier, and the scatter of broken glass. People were standing around in smaller groups now, talking excitedly. There was no sign of Stella, but he could see the woman he had spoken to, and he made for her straight-away. She looked at him rather blankly. "Your little girl? She went outside, I think, to see what was happening.

Why shouldn't she? She's quite old enough to look after herself."

Afterwards he supposed he had said something to her, it might even have been something polite. Outside there was a fairly large crowd now, standing round the heap of fallen rubble. An ambulance stood at the curb, and the attendants must be having a difficult time getting through to their patients, though they had the help now of several uniformed constables. He pushed his way to the center, where one man still lay motionless, with his head in a woman's lap. There was no sign of Stella, and somehow when he thought of her he couldn't imagine her in a press like this. If she was to stand and stare, as she admitted to doing on occasion, it would be when she was alone and could think her own thoughts without distraction.

How long would it take her to get home, supposing that was where she had gone? He thought she would have gone there, with the instinct of the wounded animal to hide itself; it was, after all, the only place she had. To be on the safe side, he'd give her half an hour. But he wasn't really comfortable until he telephoned, twenty minutes later, and found that this guess, at least, had been correct.

VII

"She was there all right when I telephoned," he told Chris and Star later. They were in the hire car again, on their way to Dr. Conway's. "I spoke to Winnie. She said Stella had come home 'all upset,' and they'd put her to bed, and the doctor had given her a sedative. So we shouldn't be able to see her again tonight."

"I don't see why you should want to," said Chris. "It's laughable, isn't it? After all our varied conjectures as to Joe's motives, that it should come down to this."

"As a matter of fact, I don't feel very much like laughing," Antony told him.

"No . . . of course. But it's obvious *now*, isn't it, that Joe had a crush on Stella almost from the time she went to live with them."

"I think she became an obsession with him," Maitland agreed somberly. Star glanced at him and asked in a subdued tone,

"Do you suppose Mrs. Baker knows?"

"I doubt it."

"I can't think what she'll say."

"Plenty, I expect. You know how it is . . . the only sins are those of the flesh."

"Poor Stella. It seems a shame she should have to bear it all alone."

"If you call being a member of the Baker household being alone—" said Maitland dryly. Chris, who seemed to be in better spirits than either of his companions, interrupted before he could complete the sentence.

"You didn't finish telling us about the explosion."

"There's not much to tell really, except that it happened."

"In your room," said Conway, and made the words sound like an accusation.

"Well . . . yes. They couldn't tell anything about the—the device that was used, not at first glance, anyway. I don't know if an expert could do any better. And they think it must have been intended to go off later, but that's guessing, too. The maid actually had her key in the door; she was probably going to turn the bed down, they do them early on Saturday and Sunday night. She's got concussion and is badly bruised, but they think she'll be all right. The people in the street fared worse, in a way; one of them's on the danger list."

"What about your belongings?"

"I still have a dressing gown, and my shaving gear, and a toothbrush. If you can lend me a clean shirt—"

"You can't go into court in those trousers," said Chris censoriously.

"If one of Bushey's colleagues on the circuit can lend me a wig and gown, I expect I can manage."

"Was yours the only room affected?"

"Everything was thrown about in the adjoining ones, but no irreparable damage, so far as I know. Luckily, the hotel isn't full. They've moved us all to the other side, and roped off the corridor, and put a tarpaulin over the hole in the wall. I can't pretend I'm really popular with the management. They seem to think it was all my fault."

"What I really want to know," said Chris, "is what the police had to say."

"There wasn't much they could say until they've pursued their enquiries a little further."

"Surely you told them—"

"The inspector was a stranger to me. For that matter, I don't think he'd been long in Arkenshaw. I told him about the car, and he said it was obviously an accident; and about Simple Simon, and he said there'd been a lot of hooliganism down by the canal. And then he asked me, humorously, if I could give him any reason why someone should be pursuing a vendetta against me, so of course I said no."

"But—"

"But what?"

"We can't go on like this," said Chris. "Something's got to be done."

"Well, I have a few ideas. I thought perhaps Inspector Duckett might be a more receptive audience for what is really pure guesswork."

"Tonight?"

"I think so, don't you?"

"You can have your dinner first," said Star. "Then I'll stay with your father, Chris, and you two can go and talk to Dad. You'll find him at the Slubbers' Arms, most like."

"It seems a bit rude to rush away like that."

"Dr. Conway won't mind," said Star, comfortably sure of herself. "So long as neither of you gets indigestion, you know."

VIII

Dr. Conway was accommodating, as always, and the plan went off without a hitch. Inspector Duckett was playing darts, and winning, but he saw Maitland and Conway almost as soon as they went in, and he joined them at a table in the corner when the game was over. "Now then," he said, when Chris had explained what had happened at the hotel. He lifted the tankard of beer which Antony had fetched from the bar while the recital was going on and said again, blankly, "Now then!"

"What we thought," said Maitland apologetically, borrowing Chris's phrase, "was that something would have to be done."

"Did you tell Inspector Middleton?"

"About the other incidents . . . yes, I did. I don't think he took me seriously."

"Now, look here—"

"It's reasonable enough from his point of view. I might be a crank, or suffering from persecution mania . . . something like that."

"That's right, too. He doesn't know," said Fred Duckett grimly, "how fain you are to get into trouble."

Maitland smiled at him, but did not attempt to argue. "Yesterday's attempts were bad enough, but there's a sort of recklessness about what happened today. Four people were hurt; they might just as easily have been killed."

153

"Someone had the means—blasting powder, or whatever—*and* was able to get into your room."

"Choose your time, and it wouldn't be difficult. There are ways of dealing with locked doors . . . I don't have to tell *you*."

"And of finding out which room you were in."

"Someone called on me at a quarter to eleven this morning, and asked the clerk to make a note to tell me a Mr. Smith had called. The slip was there, in the pigeonhole with my key. He'd only to hang about until the clerk put it there to note the room number."

"Wouldn't you have wondered, if you'd got the message before the explosion?"

"Of course I should, but I don't think I'd have imagined anything so fantastic. So there you are, if love laughs at locksmiths, so does desperation."

" 'appen you're right."

"As for the explosive, that rather reinforces the idea I had. They didn't go out and pinch it specially for this job . . . somebody had it handy."

"You'd best tell me what's on your mind."

"It's a bit complicated."

"Aye, I daresay," said the inspector dourly.

"My first thought was the same as yours, Chris. Somebody had something to hide that might come to light when we started asking questions about Joe. It wasn't until much later that I realized it might be the questions about Alfred Baker that were causing the trouble."

"But—" said Chris; but whatever he had been going to say was drowned by Inspector Duckett's protest.

"You're not telling me *he'd* been up to something shady."

"That's just what I am saying. These last two days, there's been just one thing that has kept me from giving up . . . Alfred Baker's three thousand pounds. Which is ironical, really, when it hadn't anything directly to do with the case."

"But—" said Chris again, and again he broke off as though unable to formulate his protest.

"Foster wasn't thinking straight when he assumed that Baker had saved that amount out of the four pounds a week he kept for himself. It just couldn't have been done . . . or rather, it could, if he'd saved every penny—literally every penny—for about fifteen years, which I just don't believe."

"Well, then, where did he get it from?"

"Do you remember telling me, Chris, that there had been a number of jewel robberies in Thorburndale?"

"I also told you—"

"I remember. Some nonsense about the Lady Mayoress and windows being broken at some school or other."

"I can't see that one thing is more relevant than another."

"Wait a bit! You also told me that Herbert Foster's practice was almost exclusively concerned with the county, and *he* told us that Alfred Baker dealt with most insurance matters for him."

"Well . . . yes," said Chris, as though making a great concession.

"All right, then. He'd be in a position to know, wouldn't he—Baker, I mean—which of their clients was worth robbing?"

"It's beginning to make sense," Conway agreed cautiously. He glanced at Inspector Duckett, who had been listening to this exchange in stony silence, but who now roused himself to wrathful speech.

"Nay, you're never trying to tell me, lad, that Alfred Baker—*Alfred Baker*—was in with a gang of jewel thieves."

"Is it so difficult to believe?"

"But he's—he was a *good* man."

"Not everyone that saith unto me, 'Lord, Lord'—"

"It's easy to talk," said Fred Duckett shortly.

"On the contrary, believe me; I've been giving this a good deal of thought." He watched with some sympathy while the inspector struggled with the idea that had been presented to him. "I'm not saying, you know, that he took any part in their activities; in fact, I'm quite sure he would keep deliberately away from them. But a word in season to a good friend . . . what harm could there be in that? An indiscretion, no more . . . and not his fault what use was made of the information."

"And this good friend then, *paid* him—"

"It explains a lot," said Chris. He sounded eager now. "It explains the three thousand pounds, and why someone was afraid when they knew we were asking questions, and why they didn't care whether they killed you, Antony, or just incapacitated you, because once the trial was over you wouldn't be likely to take any further interest in Arkenshaw's affairs."

"That's just how I worked it out."

"You're mad, the pair of you," said Duckett roundly.

"Are we?" He turned to Chris. "Phone Foster and ask him how many of his clients have been burgled, and get him to check with the bank how and when the payments were made into Baker's account."

"He'd have a fit."

"Then Inspector Duckett must do it . . . yes, that's a better idea, of course."

"I'll not say there mightn't be something in it," said the inspector in a grudging tone. "But supposing Baker had had a legacy now—"

"Foster would have known about it, and there was no reason why he should keep the information to himself. He was pretty open with us . . . too open, I thought at first."

"And that wouldn't explain the various attacks," Chris pointed out.

"No . . . I see. Well, grant you're right then . . . for t' sake of argument," he added quickly. "Grant you're right; who's this friend you're talking about? The man who's behind the whole thing and behind the attacks on you as well."

"The first sign that we were being kept under observation was on Friday evening . . . well, they knew we'd be in court all day. I noticed the black Volkswagen when we left Foster's house, but I daresay we were followed as we went there as well. Someone who knew I was coming to Arkenshaw. Someone who knew my name, who knew what happened when I was here before—"

"Who knew your reputation," Inspector Duckett put in, but Maitland was too engrossed in his argument to take offense.

"If you like to put it that way," he agreed. "It follows, I think, that it was someone you had made an appointment with, Chris, giving my name, so that he knew I was making enquiries, not just working to my brief. Not one of the youngsters . . . not either of the priests. There was that chap in America who was leading a double life, of course, but somehow I can't see either of them getting away with that in Arkenshaw."

"Foster himself . . . or Claud O'Donnell . . . or Peter Rawdon," said Chris, pausing hopefully between each suggestion.

"Nay now, Mr. Foster's well-respected hereabouts," Fred Duckett protested.

"Not Foster," Maitland assured him. "He wouldn't have needed to pay Baker for information about his own clients."

"Of course not, I wasn't thinking," Conway agreed. "But the other two . . . I don't see that there's a ha'penny to pick between them."

"I can only guess, of course"—Chris gave a sudden crack of laughter and then was unnaturally solemn again —"but O'Donnell's attitude was at least consistent. He was hostile to our enquiry, and he said so plainly enough. Whereas Rawdon affected sympathy with our motives, at the same time doing his best to damn Joe. I suppose he thought if he could only convince me that Joe deserved anything that was coming to him, it would put a stop to the investigation there and then."

"You went out of your way to talk about insurance," Chris reminded him.

"Well, I was hoping for some reaction, but I wasn't thinking of anything quite so drastic. There are two more points that may be worth your consideration, Inspector," he added. (Duckett's face was expressionless, there was no telling what he was thinking.) "Our appointment with Rawdon was for ten-thirty. The man who enquired at the hotel came at a quarter to eleven, when it was pretty safe to assume I'd be out of the way. The other thing is an impression only . . . it was an odd friendship, the well-to-do chartered accountant and the impecunious solicitor's clerk. Rawdon was at some pains to stress their common interests, but somehow I didn't feel that what he said rang true."

"You didn't like him," said Chris, struck by a sudden thought, "because he tried to patronize you. And neither did I," he admitted honestly.

"That's true enough, but it doesn't alter anything. What about it, Inspector. Have I made out a case?"

"Not one that would stand up in court, Mr. Maitland. I don't have to tell you that."

"A case for investigation—" His tone was light, and he let the sentence trail, but he was watching Duckett with some anxiety.

"Well now"—the inspector wasn't hurrying himself, not

for anybody—"I'm thinking if what you say about this Mr. Rawdon is right, we'll be able to find t' proof." He drank the rest of his beer and put down the tankard with a resounding clang. "I'd best be getting along to t' station," he said. "I'll telephone Mr. Foster, like you suggested, and I'll have a word with Inspector Middleton, too."

"Will he still be there?"

"Sure to be. It's a serious matter, blowing up t' Midland Hotel. And we'll have another shot at getting hold of Fennister *and* Teddy Hill. It wouldn't surprise me to learn it was him as called and asked for you, and all the rest of it."

"That's something else," said Chris, frowning. "Why bring them into it? From what I understand they're petty criminals, not up to the sort of organized robbery we've been talking about."

"They don't have the class," said Duckett, nodding his head. "Not but what I understand that part of it well enough. This Mr. Rawdon'd be a fence, I'm thinking . . . he'd have to take strong-arm stuff where he could find it."

"That's right," Antony agreed. "No self-respecting burglar would want to get involved in that. All the same, Inspector, I'm sorry we've spoiled your evening between us."

"Think nowt of it. You may have done me a good turn, Mr. Maitland, for all I know."

"I hope it works out that way."

"In t' meantime"—he paused and looked from one of them to the other—"in t' meantime, you'll both take care."

"Yes, of course." This was said far too readily to carry any real conviction, and he caught Fred Duckett's sceptical look. "They probably won't know yet that the hotel business was a washout, we'll be safe enough in court tomorrow, and after that I'll be going home."

"Let's hope you're right," said the inspector ponderously. "Let's just hope you're right."

When he had gone they had another whisky. "They'll find their proof," said Antony after a pause, rather as if Conway had been arguing with him.

"I expect they will. It's queer, you know," said Chris, suddenly becoming loquacious, "I found what you said convincing, but I can't really believe that Alfred Baker—"

"That's because you've been brainwashed on the subject of his respectability."

"Yes, I suppose it is."

"Even the children, if that's what is worrying you . . . I'm sure they started out in genuine kindness of heart, but I wouldn't like to swear they went on that way. I think the reputation they were gaining might itself prove a temptation."

"And Baker was looking forward to a cottage in the country when he retired," said Chris.

"A reasonable enough ambition, after all. And who am I to judge their motives?" said Maitland in a depressed tone. And then, more briskly, "We haven't discussed the question of Stella's evidence."

"You can't call her."

"I've done worse things than that in my time," Maitland told him, but Chris thought he looked worried and uncertain.

"Yes, but—"

"Well, I don't want to, as a matter of fact. If you can persuade Joe to give us the story instead."

"But . . . good lord . . . I never even considered—"

"Take a deep breath and start again," Antony advised him.

"*That* won't enlist the jury's sympathy."

"What won't?"

"The fact that Joe got the girl pregnant, and when he admitted it to his foster father . . . come to think of it, it would make more sense if Baker had killed *him*."

160

"Do you really think so?"

"The whole thing's insane," said Conway crossly. "I took it for granted we'd still be using Dr. Naylor's evidence, and you said yourself we wouldn't be calling Joe."

"I've changed my mind . . . or had it changed for me."

"That's all very well. It's Joe's decision, anyway."

"Need you point that out to him?"

"I suppose you've got some angle I haven't thought of yet," Conway grumbled. "What do you want me to say?"

"That Stella has told me the truth about what they discussed that afternoon, and if he won't admit it on direct examination we shall have no alternative but to call her."

"That's pretty brutal, isn't it?"

"I don't think so," said Maitland stubbornly, but again his expression belied the words.

"Have it your own way."

"I mean to." He drank the rest of his whisky and smiled at Conway's rather sulky look. "It's going to be awkward, talking to Jenny tonight."

"Will you tell her about the explosion?"

"I think I must. Simple Simon wouldn't rate the national press, but a thing like this will . . . don't you think?"

"They may not mention your name, but she knows where you're staying, of course."

"Of course." But it was no use worrying about that now. "Do you suppose you can get Anderson to agree to letting Mrs. Baker stay at home tomorrow. You can say it's because Stella's ill—"

"Good lord, yes. We don't want her there to complicate matters. But she'll have to know sooner or later."

"Sooner, I think. I was wondering . . . it's a big thing to ask, but do you think Star would tell her?"

"I . . . yes, I'm sure she would." He paused, thinking it over. "Something will have to be arranged about Stella, if Mrs. Baker cuts up rough."

161

"You know, I've an idea Sister Mary Dominic might be helpful there."

"Star can't talk to a nun about people having babies," said Conway in a horrified tone.

"You think not? I'll have a bet with you, if you like, that neither of them would turn a hair. Star's like Jenny . . . she'd tackle a dragon any day if she thought it would do some good."

"And Sister Mary Dominic?"

"I just think she's not quite—not quite so unworldly as you seem to suppose." He glanced at his glass regretfully, as though considering the advisability of having a refill, and then said resolutely, "Are you coming with me to see Grandma?"

"I didn't think you'd want to see her now."

"Well, yes, I think I should."

"I don't see—"

"You will." He came to his feet as he spoke and stood waiting while Conway hurriedly emptied his glass. "It's getting late, we'd better go right away or she may have gone to bed."

He looked around carefully when they left the pub, but there was no sign of the black Volkswagen. He hadn't really expected it to be there.

IX

If old Mrs. Duckett was surprised to see them, she didn't show it. She let them in and led the way back into the kitchen again; and if she noticed that Maitland was holding himself rather more stiffly than usual, as was his habit when his shoulder was painful, she didn't say anything about that, either. But when she had sent Chris out to the scullery to fill the heavy iron kettle she fixed her eyes critically on Antony and said in a belligerent tone, "Now then! You're worried about something. I can see that."

It was queer how in her company all the minor irritations fell away, leaving only the principal cause of his apprehension clear in his mind. He smiled at her and said lightly, "You don't approve of gambling, do you?"

"I do not." He didn't think for a moment that she was deceived by his tone. She had gone back to her favorite place in the Windsor chair at the left of the hearth, and couldn't have looked more regal, Antony considered, if she'd been Queen Victoria herself. He looked at her for a moment and then turned his eyes to the leaping flames.

"I'm going to take a chance, tomorrow in court."

"A chance . . . does he deserve it?"

"I think, perhaps, he does."

"It's his life you're gambling with," said Grandma. If she didn't sound approving, she didn't exactly sound condemnatory, either, but he said eagerly, as though trying to justify himself,

"No more of a chance than a surgeon takes with a tricky operation."

"Then what are you fidgeting about?" There was no trace of sympathy in her tone.

"I'm not sure if I'm justified—" He let the sentence trail into silence as Chris came between them to place the kettle on the hob. "A lot of people are going to be hurt, and if I'm wrong they'll have been hurt for nothing."

"And if you're right?"

"The difference between a life sentence and three years —perhaps—for manslaughter." He hesitated, and spread his hands in an oddly defenseless gesture. "He's so young."

"I don't hold with murder," said Grandma uncompromisingly.

"Nor do I. I just meant . . . too young to cope with a passionate attachment. I think really it amounted to an obsession—"

"Romeo and Juliet stuff," said Chris, who had taken a chair between them, where he could keep an eye on the kettle's activities. Grandma said slowly, as though she was puzzled,

"You're talking about feelings. That lot in court, wouldn't they want facts?"

"If I could make them see—" He broke off, frowning. "Uncle Nick could do it better."

"Well, he isn't here, and he couldn't help you if he was," said old Mrs. Duckett, at her most forthright. "You think you've found out why t' lad did it, I can see that, even if you are talking in riddles. But what I don't see, young man, is why you've brought your problem to me."

"I want your help."

"Well now, let's see. If it was something easy you'd have gone straight to t' point," said Grandma shrewdly, "instead of dithering about like this."

Maitland laughed. There wasn't much amusement to be found in the situation, but Grandma was as good as a tonic any day. "You're quite right, of course. I want you to answer a question for me, and you're not going to like it."

"Why not?" she asked sharply, and scowled at him.

"You've always told me, you don't hold with scurrilous talk."

"No more I do."

"Well, will you . . . forget about that for a minute, and help me?"

"I don't know about that." She sat looking at him somberly. The kettle began to sing, and Chris got up, unnoticed by either of his companions, and went to the cupboard for cups and saucers, and then came back to spoon tea into the brown pot that was keeping warm above the range. "You haven't reminded me I owe you a favor," the old lady said, and was surprised when Maitland flushed. But he only said steadily,

"There's no need to talk of favors between you and me, Grandma."

"No more there is. But Joe Hartley's nowt to me," she told him roughly.

"I think if I could explain to you—"

"No need of that." She held up a hand to stop him. "I'll answer your question," she said, and heard him take a deep breath, as though of relief.

"It's very simple really," he said. "When I came here the other evening and asked you about the Bakers you said, 'I don't hold with scandal.' "

"No more I do."

"Well, then, that's the question." He leaned forward a little, but his voice was deliberately expressionless, hiding his eagerness. "That's what I want to know, Grandma. Why did you say that?"

∧ Monday, 23rd May

On Monday morning the town was buzzing with specula-
tion about the explosion, but by some miracle Maitland's
name had escaped mention in the newspapers. By contrast, the atmosphere in the court seemed apathetic, and
there was a handful of people only on the public benches.
Maitland, rising to open for the defense, had to struggle
against the prevailing feeling—as clear to him as if someone had shouted it aloud—that the case was as good as
over. Joe was looking rather more sullen than before,
which might or might not be a mask for nervousness. Chris
Conway reported that he had agreed, though not without
a struggle, to answer Maitland's questions, and to do so
without prevarication; it remained to be seen whether he
would be equally compliant when he got into the witness
box, but, "I think he'll cooperate," Chris had said uneasily.
"He seems to regard it as a sort of bargain we've made
between us." Mrs. Baker wasn't in court; most likely Star
was with her already. When all was said and done, Star
had probably the hardest part of all to play.

But beneath all these surface thoughts one question
repeated itself relentlessly in Maitland's mind: was the
chance he was taking justified, or not? A lot of people
(that was an echo, too, of his talk with Grandma) were
going to be hurt.

There wasn't much to be said, which was just as well
. . . he wasn't in the mood to speak at length, and in any
event the case depended scarcely at all on what he said
now, or did not say. Joe's evidence was all-important, the
manner of its presentation perhaps even more so than the
matter. It remained to be seen what kind of an impression
he would make upon the jury.

The judge had retreated into a coma again; he'd come
out of it fast enough if anything was said that wasn't
crystal clear. Anderson had a self-satisfied look. He'd dealt
with his part of the business thoroughly—perhaps even too
thoroughly, but that was a matter of opinion—on Friday.
The presentation of the case for the defense could hold no
terrors for him, though he permitted himself a faint look
of surprise on hearing that Joe Hartley was the only witness to be called. It must seem to him that they were
virtually throwing in their hand. Well, there was still a
trick or two to play for. Maitland finished what he had to
say, and remained standing while the prisoner was
escorted from the dock to the witness-box. He was aware
of Bushey, beside him, unruffled as ever; of Conway's tension; of the discomfort of a borrowed wig that was too
tight for him, just as the gown he was wearing was short
and loose across the shoulders. He saw the Douay Bible
produced again, and heard Joe repeating the words of the
oath, his voice low-pitched, but his tone unexpectedly
firm and clear. Perhaps, after all . . .

The preliminary questions. Take them quickly enough
not to bore the jury, slowly enough to reassure the witness.
"Your full name is Joseph William Hartley . . . you reside
at ten Cartwright Avenue—"

"Well, I did," said Joe. He had no means of telling, of
course, how much preferable a simple affirmative would
have been. "I don't suppose I could ever go back there,
could I?"

167

A too literal interpretation of the words of the oath? A desire to please that was surprising when you considered his attitude at the earlier interviews? Or simply concern for Stella, the fear that his lawyers might break their promise and call the child to give evidence after all? "You did reside there, didn't you, until the time of your arrest?"

"That's right."

"And you are seventeen years old?"

"Seventeen and nine months. I'll be eighteen in August."

"Thank you." (When I want him to amplify his statements he'll become tongue-tied, but that's the way things go.) "You are an orphan, and you have lived since you were four years old in the home of Mr. and Mrs. Alfred Baker, as their foster child."

"Yes, I—"

"You looked on them as your parents?"

"In a manner of speaking."

Mr. Justice Gilmour raised his head. "I do not wish to embarrass you, Mr. Maitland" (damn it all, can't he see the boy's nervous?) "but I should like some clarification of that last remark."

"The witness was agreeing with my statement, my lord."

"He regarded Alfred Baker as his father and Mrs. Agnes Baker as his mother?"

"So I believe," said Maitland, and looked to Joe for confirmation. "Is that right?"

"Yes, sir—my lord." He sounded confused now. Maitland put his next question in what he hoped was a bracing tone.

"In the same way you looked on their other foster children as your brothers and sisters?"

"Yes."

"You were the third of the children in age, weren't you? The third to be taken into the household."

"I was."

"And of the younger children, most of them came into Mr. and Mrs. Baker's care in infancy."

"Most of them. Yes."

"Did something happen two years ago to change this pattern of events?"

"In a sort of way."

Another opening for Gilmour? "Please tell us, in your own words—" Maitland invited, repressing a strong desire to glance in the judge's direction.

"Well, there was Stella." He was more cautious now, but still more open than Maitland had hoped.

"What about Stella?" he prompted.

"She was . . . different," said Joe.

"In what way?"

"Well, for one thing, she was older than the other kids had been when they came to us."

"How old was she at that time?"

"Eleven."

"Do you remember the first time you saw her?"

"Of course I do." Joe's tone was firmer now. "I came home from school, and she was there. She had a blue dress on, and she'd been crying. Well, it was no wonder, really. Her own people hadn't been dead all that long."

"Did her coming make any difference to the family?"

"Not really."

"To you personally?"

"Well, I got this idea she wanted someone to look after her," said Joe confidingly. He seemed for the moment to have forgotten that there was anyone in court but himself and his counsel. If there was any way at all of keeping it like that . . .

"You said she was 'different.' Can you tell me of what this difference consisted?"

"She was shy, sort of. She wasn't used to a crowd."

"Did this shyness persist?"

"I suppose you could say it did. She never seemed to settle down, not properly."

"Was anyone unkind to her?"

"Not to say unkind. Mum used to get a bit impatient. Said she was always daydreaming. Stella wasn't doing any harm."

"And the younger members of the family?" He caught Mr. Justice Gilmour's eye. "I am speaking of them as a family, my lord, to avoid confusion. I mean, of course, Mr. and Mrs. Baker's foster children."

"Thank you, Mr. Maitland," said the judge, closing his eyes again. Maitland turned back to the witness.

"You were going to tell us—"

"They'd tease her. Not meaning anything, I suppose."

"Did Stella get used to that?"

"No, she never did. She'd believe all sorts of nonsense, even when I told her it wasn't true."

"You didn't like to see her worried?"

"It wasn't fair."

"I'm sure this is all very interesting, my lord," said Anderson, coming to his feet, "but is it really relevant?"

"Is it relevant, Mr. Maitland?"

"I shall demonstrate its relevance in due course, if your lordship pleases."

"Very well." He waved a tired hand, presumably by way of invitation to continue. Anderson subsided.

Counsel for the Defense looked back at his client again. He was nervous himself now. Chris would realize that, but perhaps no one else . . . "You have told us that Stella's arrival in the family made some difference to your own way of life."

Joe was silent for an appreciable moment, his eyes fixed, frowning, on Maitland's face. "Of course it did, in a way," he said. "I'd take her about a bit, walks and that; she seemed to like walking. Or perhaps it was just that it got her out of the way of the others."

"She didn't fit in?"

"There'd always be some ragging. She was different, you know," said Joe again, giving the word the same almost caressing intonation as he had done before. "More sensitive," he added, by way of explanation. "It frightened her."

"So you did your best to stand between her and the rougher edges of life." He waited for some comment, but Joe just stood looking at him, so after a while he went on, "Was there any other way in which her coming made a difference to you?"

"I'd try to be around at home more. I'd try to head Freddie off . . . he's the worst for teasing."

"You thought about Stella a good deal, one way and another."

"Yes, I did. Why shouldn't I?"

"No reason at all." He was intent on the witness now, alert to the sudden truculence in his voice, Mr. Justice Gilmour's wasplike interruptions of the examination momentarily forgotten. "What I want to establish is whether this protective attitude of yours intensified as time wore on, so that Stella came perhaps to be the most important thing in your life."

Again that was something that needed thinking over. "She *was* important," Joe said at last.

"More important than your work, or your recreation; more important than your family and your friends?"

"She needed someone to look after her."

"And, as you saw it, that was a job for you."

"There wasn't anybody else."

"I see." Was that enough for the jury or wasnt' it? Could they possibly understand . . . ? "Will you tell me now about the day your foster father died?"

171

"*All* day?"

"From the time you sat down to dinner at about one o'clock."

"You mean, when we talked about our plans for the afternoon?"

"That will do quite well."

"Dad always liked to know what we were doing. I said I'd take Stella for a walk. And Win said she didn't need her for the washing up, so that was all right."

"You did, in fact, go out together?"

This time his hesitation was very marked. "Yes. We got the tram to Lane's End and walked on the moor."

"Did something happen in the course of your walk?"

"Not to say happen."

"Did Stella confide in you . . . something that was worrying her?"

"Mr. Maitland, you must not lead your witness."

"As your lordship pleases." But he hardly noticed the rebuke, he was as tense now as Joe was. "You had some conversation in the course of this walk?"

"My lord!" Anderson was on his feet again. Maitland turned quickly.

"I must ask your indulgence, my lord. The only alternative would be to call the child as a witness, and naturally I do not wish to do that."

"I see. You realize that if I allow this line of questioning to continue you will be asking the court to rely on your client's word alone."

"I must rely on the perception of the jury, my lord, to see the truth."

"Very well. I am inclined to grant the defense a certain amount of latitude, Mr. Anderson."

"As your lordship pleases." He seemed more puzzled than upset by the decision. Maitland turned back to his witness again. "You were going to tell us about your con-

172

versation with Stella on the afternoon of April twenty-fourth."

"We didn't talk much at first—" He broke off there, and for a moment Maitland thought he was going to have to do some more prompting. The question was how much he could get away with in that line without having Gilmour change his mind. But then Joe went on, only this time he was speaking in a low voice, not clearly at all, "She told me she was going to have a baby."

"What?" said the judge, sitting up suddenly.

"She told me she was going to have a baby," Joe repeated, his tone as brittle as glass.

"Am I to understand that this evidence is tending to show motive, Mr. Maitland?"

"It is, my lord."

"And that you"—he was addressing the prisoner directly now—"are the father of this—this young girl's child?"

This time there was no need for prompting, or for asking Joe to speak up. He said quite loudly, and certainly belligerently, "No, of course I'm not. Didn't you understand that I worship the ground she walks on? I wouldn't do anything to hurt her."

(In the pause that followed Maitland heard his instructing solicitor say, quite distinctly, that he'd *said* he didn't approve of Joe's taste in literature.)

"In that case I do not see that it has anything to do with the matter in hand at all," said his lordship firmly, and again Joe spoke up; if there had been a bargain he was going to keep his side of it, and he took the words out of his counsel's mouth.

"Of course it is," he said, with a kind of scorn that anyone should need so obvious a fact explained to them. "It was Dad's baby . . . Alfred Baker's baby. He shouldn't have done that to Stella. That's why I killed him."

⋀ Epilogue

"But you can't leave it there," said Jenny reproachfully, when he had reached this point in his narrative the following evening and had broken off as though admiring the dramatic quality of the last statement. "For one thing, you haven't told me what happened to Joe."

"He got three years for manslaughter. If he goes on studying law, Chris's senior partner has promised him his articles when he comes out. He won't be quite twenty, even then."

"You must have made a good speech," said Jenny, with something in her tone as near to irony as she was ever likely to come. Antony grinned at her.

"The speech of a lifetime," he agreed. "No, seriously, I think the jury could recognize sincerity when they heard it, and there was no doubt that Joe was sincere."

"But they can't have left it there . . . in court, I mean."

"They didn't. They were far too full of curiosity by that time, and as it would have been manifestly improper for me to continue with a line of questioning based on hearsay, Gilmour took over the examination himself."

"What did Joe tell him?"

"It isn't a nice story, Jenny."

"No, but I want to hear."

He picked up his cup and drank some coffee before he

continued. "It took some doing to get Stella to tell him the whole thing, and when she had done he could hardly believe it, except that it was so circumstantial that he *had* to, if you understand me."

"I think I do."

"It seems that one day at the beginning of February— it was a Monday, Joe said—Mrs. Baker had taken the whole family, from Freddie down, to the skating rink in town. Except Stella."

"I should have thought the little ones would be too small to skate."

"I don't know. Perhaps they got their fun some other way. It doesn't matter at all. George had a date, and Winnie and Joe were going skating, too, as soon as they got off from work. But Alfred Baker was going straight home and wanted his tea in good time, because of his chess game with Peter Rawdon. So Stella was left at home to take care of his needs. I daresay she wasn't as keen on skating as the rest of them."

"But I still don't understand . . . after all, she was only thirteen."

"You haven't seen her, Jenny. She got Joe pretty well stirred up, only fortunately she roused his chivalrous instincts. This didn't come out in court, of course, but Grandma told me that there's been a lot of talk in Arkenshaw about Alfred Baker and his affairs, though it was never too open because of charity covering a multitude of sins, I suppose. I'd pretty well realized what must have happened before I saw her . . . I mean, it was Joe who was angry and went looking for his foster father, not the other way round. But without her confirmation I doubt if I'd have had the nerve to try to bring it out in court."

"Joe could have told you."

"That was the trouble. The only way we could persuade him to talk was by pretending we knew everything he could tell us anyway. If he'd realized we were only guessing, he'd have kept his mouth shut, and we could have whistled for our evidence."

"Poor Stella. And poor Mrs. Baker. How dreadful for them."

"The whole thing makes me sick," said Antony and got up and walked to the window and back again. "But if Joe had been convicted of murder, and got a life sentence, he'd have had much less chance of making good when he came out of prison."

"Yes, I realize that."

He smiled down at her. "If you really try, I daresay you can find plenty to sympathize with in Alfred Baker, too. I wonder how he felt about not having children of his own. I mean, he obviously wanted some or he'd hardly have embarked on one or two, let alone thirteen foster children."

"It all seems so contradictory. Not only the baby, but the jewel robberies, too."

"People are, love. Haven't you noticed? But perhaps he was more of a mix-up than the rest of us. I mean, there he was, enjoying his reputation, but there was his old age to provide for and that country cottage he had his eye on. You'd have noticed, too, if you'd been with us, that the children had had it pretty well drilled into them that they ought to be grateful; and Joe knew all about his mother's intemperate habits, which could have been kept from him easily enough, I should think."

Jenny sighed and accepted the cup he was holding out to her. "You didn't finish telling me what happened in court."

"Well, Joe was talking more freely by this time; he wanted us to understand that what had happened hadn't been Stella's fault. There she was, alone in the house, and Baker came in wanting his tea, and she'd gone into one of her daydreams, or started reading a book, or something, and had forgotten all about it. He seemed to be very put out and told her to go up to her bedroom, he'd get something for himself. And she thought he was going to beat her, because that was one of the things Freddie had told her would happen if she didn't behave, and she'd believed him. So when Alfred Baker came upstairs and was kind to her instead . . . I'll leave the rest to your imagination. But it's rather pathetic that she told Joe she thought a sort of miracle would take place afterwards, and everything would be all right forever."

"Poor Stella," said Jenny again and picked up the coffeepot, apparently without any idea of what she was going to do with it. "What will become of her?"

"She's with Star Conway at the moment. Star said Stella was her namesake and she was going to look after her until something better could be arranged. And Sister Mary Dominic is taking an interest; I expect the nuns would know somewhere she could go. That was probably the most valiant thing Star did, after Grandma brought her up as a good Methodist."

"What was?"

"Braving the terrors of the convent to enlist their sympathy. But I don't envy her the task of breaking the news to Mrs. Baker, either."

Jenny shuddered, but even her ready sympathy was not engaged to the exclusion of curiosity. "What happened when Joe went in to see Mr. Baker and told him what Stella had said?" she asked, and filled the cup and passed it back to him. Antony placed it on the mantelpiece and remained standing with his back to the empty grate.

"Well, at first he tried to say Joe was lying, that he was responsible for the girl's condition himself. But when Joe wouldn't buy that he admitted it at last and offered Joe money to say the child was his . . . 'to save your mother's feelings, you owe her that at least.' And that, I think (but Joe wasn't too clear about the sequence of events) was when he picked up the poker."

"How horrible!"

"Not really an enjoyable episode." But then a more pleasant thought struck him. "There are two people who are pleased with the way things have turned out, though. Father O'Brien, for one, because Joe sent a message that he'd like to see him."

"And the other?"

"Inspector Duckett."

"You mean everything about the jewel robberies is working out as you said."

"Yes, it is." He thought about that for a moment. "But not because I said it, if you see what I mean."

"I don't quite—"

"They picked up Harry Fennister and the other chap, and Harry talked. Not about the robberies themselves, of course, he didn't know anything about them, but they got enough out of him to justify asking for a search warrant for Peter Rawdon's house, and what they found makes it pretty certain he's been in business as a receiver for some time. I got all this from the inspector on the telephone this morning before I left Arkenshaw, so I'm afraid I haven't any details. But I'm glad that at least those two are satisfied with the way things have gone."

"And Grandma is, too, I expect."

"Yes, do you know what she said to me? 'We'll be seeing our Fred a superintendent if you come to Arkenshaw much more.' Not that it's true, of course, but I found it consoling."

"I like the Ducketts," said Jenny in a reflective tone. "All the same, I hope you won't be going back to Arkenshaw. Not for a long time."